Her medical instincts were good.

He'd bet she could cure an elephant of a head cold if she tried. Her ministrations today had eased his pain and helped his wounds.

"There," she said, finishing up. "Now all it needs is a dressing. And a man who'll take care of it, instead of ripping it open, working on his bike."

She sent him a daggered look.

And Luke was ready to promise her anything.

"Thank you," he said.

"It was nothing."

Her voice was low and sweet, a velvet whisper in the small room. And Luke's resolve developed a major crack. Her lips were close, too close— and he had to taste them. Had to know if they tasted as sultry as they looked at the moment. He lowered his mouth to hers. Just a taste, he promised himself.

Just a taste.

Dear Reader,

I've always loved the American Southwest, and this book cried out to be set there. There is a magic in the rugged, untamed, high-desert region, from the deepest blue of the sky to the red dust of the soil, from the fiery sunsets to the brilliance of the stars at night.

Luke and Mariah's story is one of challenges. Can a man and a woman with divergent lives find a love to last a lifetime? Can they overcome great odds and triumph in the end?

I enjoy writing—and reading—books that embrace love and family, books that light a special spark in the reader's soul and won't let go until the final page. I think *A Family Practice* is one such book and I hope you enjoy reading it as much as I loved writing it.

Gayle Kasper

T37873

A FAMILY PRACTICE

GAYLE KASPER

SPECIAL EDITION

Published by Silhouette Books

America's Publisher of Contemporary Romance

SILHOUETTE BOOKS

ISBN-13: 978-0-373-24848-3
ISBN-10:   0-373-24848-2

A FAMILY PRACTICE

Copyright © 2007 by Gayle Kasper

Visit Silhouette Books at www.eHarlequin.com

Printed in U.S.A.

Books by Gayle Kasper

Silhouette Special Edition

A Family Practice #1848

Books written under the pseudonym Gayle Kaye

Silhouette Romance

Hard Hat and Lace #925
His Delicate Condition #961
Daddy Trouble #1014
Bachelor Cop #1177
Daddyhood #1227
Sheriff Takes a Bride #1359

Harlequin Duets

Kiss That Cowboy #60

GAYLE KASPER

After a long and varied career in nursing, Gayle Kasper hung up her stethoscope to write romances. She's received numerous awards for her books, including nominations for a Texas Gold, *Romantic Times BOOKreviews* and a Golden Heart Award. She's a member of RWA and the Land of Enchantment Romance Authors.

A Midwesterner from Kansas, Gayle now lives in Santa Fe, New Mexico, where she says, "My soul belongs." She's been married for thirty years to her own real-life hero, who's always encouraged her writing career. In addition to writing, Gayle loves reading, gardening and playing tourist around her adopted hometown.

Gayle loves to hear from her readers. You can write to her at gaylekasper@juno.com.

In memory of the real-life Una
and all you taught me

Chapter One

Dr. Luke Phillips leaned his big silver Harley into the curve, racing the wind, and sometimes winning. It was the only pleasure he allowed himself.

He'd left the interstate behind somewhere south of Flagstaff, Arizona, preferring the solitude of this two-lane road to nowhere. Flowering cacti, the brutal sun and red rock kept him company. Dry red dust peppered his face and arms. He tasted its grit.

At the moment he'd sell his soul for the sight of a shade tree—or what passed for shade in this part of the country. Not that his soul was worth a whole hell of a lot these days.

He'd left who and what he was behind in Chicago forever.

Then a short distance ahead he spotted a small sliver of shade produced by one scrawny pine tree. He coasted the bike to a stop at the side of the road and dismounted.

Soon he'd have to consider traveling at night and sleeping by day. The afternoon sun could be relentless, even dangerous to the uninitiated. And he supposed he was that, despite the deep tan the last thousand miles or so had given him.

He sprinted across the dry bed of an arroyo and scaled the rocky mesa, intent on reaching that shade tree. A twenty-minute power nap and he'd be as good as new.

But a short distance from the tree he paused, finding the scenery had just improved—in the form of one very feminine, denim-clad fanny raised to the sky. The woman was leaning out over the edge of the rocky ledge, reaching for something a distant grasp away, oblivious to his approach behind her.

He wondered if the view from the front was half as intriguing. His gaze remained riveted on her, his breath caught halfway to his lungs as she leaned out farther over the lip of the rock.

Damn!

One stiff breeze could send her over the side.

He stood stock-still, not wanting to startle her into taking a misguided plunge. He didn't mean to gape, but since any sudden movement could bring on disaster, what else did he have to do with his time?

Time—he had plenty of that.

The entire remainder of his life, in fact.

He wasn't going back to Chicago. There was nothing there for him anymore. The medical center and trauma unit would do well without him. They had good doctors, the best.

Luke should know.

He'd been one of them himself—until two months ago.

A knot formed in his throat, but he fought it down, fought down the damning memories, as well. Life went on. It just went on without him now.

But that was the way Luke wanted it.

He didn't know how many miles he'd ridden, how many highways he'd taken. All he knew was that not one of them had brought him the solace he desired, the amnesia for his soul.

The unrelenting sun beat down, making him eager for that quick siesta in the shade, but he didn't dare move until the woman with the provocative fanny quit her trapeze act and righted herself. Besides, did he want to miss that first glimpse of her when she got up from her knees and turned around?

He wondered if her eyes were brown and earthy. Or maybe the azure-blue of the Arizona sky overhead. He imagined high cheekbones caressed by the sun, lips that curved gracefully into a smile, or maybe a feminine pout.

Just then she inched back from the mesa's precarious edge and stood up. Her hair was dark and silken and tumbled over one shoulder in a long, loose braid. In her right hand she held a plant, its roots dangling with red soil and rock, small reddish blossoms sprouting in profusion, protected by pale, spiny leaves.

"You risked your life for a damned flower?"

She spun around to face him.

He'd been wrong. Her eyes were green—and at the moment, wide with surprise at the sight of a stranger in front of her.

She obviously hadn't expected to find company out here in the middle of solitude. She drew the flower closer to her body, clutching it as if she expected he might snatch it from her.

Her frame was slight, her legs long and straight, the kind of legs that could make any red-blooded male dream of them wrapped around him during a night of hot passion.

His hands could span her tiny waist and cup the modest fullness of her high, firm breasts. The sun had given color to the tip of her nose, and a smudge of red dirt decorated the tip of her fighting chin. She nervously moistened her full, lower lip and eyed him warily.

"I didn't mean to startle you," he said gently.

He didn't want her to bolt like a frightened deer. He'd be happy to go on looking at her until this time tomorrow.

Or a month from tomorrow.

One thing he was certain of, they didn't grow women this earthy back in Chicago. Maybe it was something in the water.

Or the red dust.

She seemed to be one with the land, comfortable with it, mistress of it, and he found he liked that.

She took his measure, too, assessing his strong-built body, the width of his square shoulders, then glanced quickly in the direction he'd come, spotting the big Harley he'd left by the side of the road.

"I stopped to find some shade," he explained, not entirely sure why he was doing so.

Her eyes darted back to him, roaming over his wind-burned face, settling finally on his mouth curved in a crooked half smile he hoped passed for friendly and nonthreatening.

It seemed to.

She gave a soft, returning smile. "There's not much shade around here. You have to find it where you can."

Her voice was low, soft, innocent—and it did dangerous things to his libido.

Luke didn't reply, only continued to watch her with steady deliberation, taking in her earthy beauty, her quiet ways—and liking what he saw.

Just then she reached for the brightly woven basket at her feet and dropped the flower into it, a basket he noticed contained other plants and what looked like a jumble of old roots and bark.

"I…I should go," she said finally. "Goodbye. Enjoy your shade."

"Wait—"

She glanced up, and her gaze locked with his, one feminine brow raised questioningly.

He didn't want her to leave, disappearing from his life as if she'd been nothing more than a mirage in the desert. "You didn't answer my question—what's so special about a flower you have to lean out over the edge to dig up?"

She glanced down at the basket she held and toyed with a delicate bloom. "It's not really a flower. It's wild germander, an herb—and rare in this part of the high country."

"And rare makes it special enough to risk falling off the side of a mesa?"

He thought he saw a shadow of pain cross her delicate features. Luke knew about pain, both personally and professionally, knew how it ate at a man's soul. *His* soul.

She pinched off a blossom and raised it to her nose,

sniffing its scent. "It's special for its…medicinal value," she said, then her chin rose. "I really do have to go."

She took a step, but again Luke stopped her. "What's your name?"

She hesitated as if trying to decide if it were proper to introduce herself to a man she met on a mesa in the middle of nowhere. After a moment trust won out. She gave him a slight smile. "Mariah," she said.

"Mariah." He repeated it after her, liking its lilt, its music. It would slide easily off a man's tongue during a night of lovemaking. "I'm Luke," he offered. "Luke Phillips."

He deliberately didn't mention the doctor part. He wasn't sure he could claim the right—or that he wanted to. All his finely honed skills had failed him the one night they had mattered the most.

Now they were of no use to him.

"Hello, Luke Phillips," she answered. There was a slight hesitancy to her soft voice, something he could understand, given the circumstances.

But there was something quiet, serene, about her. Something that gave him peace somehow. Was it a part of who she was? Or something she had perfected? Whichever, he liked that about her—and wished he could find some for himself.

"Tell me about its medicinal value, this…this wild germander."

Mariah Cade studied the man in front of her. She wasn't afraid of him—though she had been at first. Just a little. Or maybe she'd just been surprised at seeing him. She seldom ran across another living soul when she was out gathering her herbs.

It was her quiet time—time to take stock of her life, perhaps wish things could be different, *better*. Better for Callie. She'd do anything to find the right herbs for her daughter, whether they grew on the side of a mesa or the far side of the moon.

She considered how best to answer the man, whose very shadow dwarfed her with its size. He had shoulders as wide as a mountain, a broad, densely muscled chest, lean hips and a strength, a potent masculinity that emanated from him like shimmers of heat off the desert plain.

His face commanded a woman's attention, with its strong Nordic features that hinted at a ruthless Viking or two in his ancestry—steel-blue eyes, a straight proud nose, square chin and a mane of brown hair, tipped blond by the sun. His skin, too, showed the kiss of sunshine, his body glistening like gold dust.

"It's an herb with many uses," she said, not sure she wanted to reveal more to this stranger. Perhaps she was protecting Callie, perhaps herself.

She hadn't missed the smile that had played at the edges of his mouth, a smile that played there now, as if he might be mocking her and her simplistic ways.

She ran a finger down a long entwined root, secure in her knowledge that this would help Callie, which was the important thing. The *only* thing, she thought as her daughter's bright smile flickered through her mind.

Callie was her life, had been from the moment she'd been conceived. They were bound together as tightly as two people could be.

"Plants can cure," she said, her voice low and wispy. "And sometimes they bring peace and calm."

Peace.

Calm.

Luke could use a little of both in his life—and he wondered if this small slip of a woman had somehow cornered the market on them both, if she held the key there in her basket of jumbled roots and flowers.

He was tempted to stick around and find out—but he lived in a world of reality. A painful reality. And the only cure for it was to keep moving. Where, he didn't know. Or care. Anywhere would do, if it eased his pain; if it made him forget—even a little.

His gaze skimmed over her, taking in her appealing curves in her dusty jeans and soft red blouse. Small Indian beads dangled from her earlobes in a spill of silver and bright color—and he longed to reach out and touch them.

Touch *her*.

If only to assure himself she was real—and not a dream his tired mind had conjured up.

Her shoulders were slight, her spine straight as a new sapling, and he had the feeling she could move over the terrain as easily as the white-tailed deer he'd glimpsed from the road as he'd passed through this high-desert land.

"So, are you off to gather more plants?" he asked, wondering if she took a siesta to escape the afternoon heat—or if she were somehow immune to it.

She checked the level of the sun, judging her time from it the way others would consult a watch. "Yes— for a little while yet."

She turned to leave. Again Luke wanted to keep her with him, but he had no reason to, at least no logical reason. He was merely passing through and their paths had crossed.

He watched her go, tripping off down the trail in her soft moccasins. He wondered what—or who—might be waiting for her at home.

A husband?

A child?

But that, he knew, was none of his business.

At least for a little while she'd made him forget his pain. And that was something no one had been able to do for him these past dark, *empty* months.

A few hours later Mariah's basket was full to over-flowing. Indian fig, wild licorice, comfrey root. Mariah was pleased to have found them all. It had been a good day. She now had enough herbs to last for a while.

She turned and started back toward the ancient truck she'd parked down by the stream that flowed briskly in the spring, fed by the snowmelt from the high mountains.

When summer came, it would dry up to dust and rock, but for now there was enough cool water to splash over her face and arms before she began her drive home.

She'd strayed farther than she'd intended today, but the hope of finding more plants had lured her on. Many of the herbs she needed were scarce in this high-desert region, but Mariah would search until she found that one lone plant. And when she couldn't find what she needed, she'd substitute.

Una Roanhorse had taught her well. The old Hopi woman's eyes were failing now—she could no longer gather roots and plants for herself, so Mariah shared what she had with her. In return, Una looked after Callie. It was a good arrangement. Callie loved the older woman, loved the Hopi tales Una often told her, the same tales Mariah had heard as a child growing up on the land of her people.

Mariah's father had been a *bahana,* a white man. She didn't remember him, though. He hadn't bothered to stay around. Her mother had died many years before, and Mariah had strayed from the native ways—not feeling like a *bahana,* not feeling entirely Hopi, either.

She'd known very little about the plants and herbs the earth gave, or how beneficial they could be. Not until she'd needed them—for Callie.

Mariah was grateful to Una for sharing her knowledge. The herbals helped Callie as nothing else had been able to do.

Certainly not the doctors' medicines.

Una had become a friend when Mariah moved here two years ago. Mariah's marriage to Will Cade had ended, probably even before he'd left for California and the new life he wanted for himself.

A life without the responsibilities of a wife or child.

A sick child.

She'd been frightened then—and alone. Except for Callie. Una had made her feel welcome, even taken her under her wing until Mariah was able to recover her pride and put her life on a steady footing.

She seldom thought of the past now, her marriage, or the man who'd abandoned them with so little regard for their welfare.

The herbs that she gathered for Callie soon became a

source of livelihood for her, a way to support herself and her daughter. She began by preparing and packaging the extras she collected and selling them to the local people. Last year she started her own mail-order business, reaching even more people with her natural medicines.

It wasn't a lot of money—her only large account was a health-food store in Phoenix—but it was enough to provide a modest living for them. And even a few extras now and then.

Just then she neared the place where she'd encountered the man on the mesa, the man with the golden body and the storm-blue eyes.

Luke.

She wasn't sure why he intrigued her, but he had. She wondered where he'd come from—and where he was headed on that big cycle of his. Not many people strayed this far from the interstate. She might have asked him, but she'd needed to get on with what she was doing. She didn't like to be away from Callie too long.

She glanced down the road, shading her eyes, curious to see if his cycle was still parked where it had been, but it was gone. She denied the quick pang of disappointment she felt, calling herself foolish for the weakness. She was no longer a schoolgirl with silly ideas in her head, but a woman, a mother—with a child who needed her.

She shifted the basket to her other hip and continued on, but Luke Phillips wasn't easily dispelled from her mind. Sunrise was a town that had been forgotten by time, passed over by the tourist trade, though it could well boast of some of Arizona's most breathtaking scenery. They didn't get very many strangers passing through—but that was no reason this man should have such a hold on her.

Perhaps it had been that indefinable look she'd glimpsed in his eyes, as if he, too, carried a pain he found difficult to bear, a pain that tore at his heart.

The way Callie did hers.

Then over the next rise Mariah stopped in her tracks. There'd been an accident. The shiny silver of a motorcycle glinted back at her, looking like a fallen warrior as it lay on its side in the center of the road.

Where was Luke?

Was he hurt?

She swiftly scanned both sides of the road, then spotted him sitting under a lone cottonwood a few yards away. "Luke," she called out to him. "What happened? Are you all right?"

He turned at the sound of her voice and she approached warily. The right side of his face was dirty and bloody. The denim of his right pant leg was ripped and he'd stripped off his black T-shirt and tied it around his thigh to stop the bleeding that was already beginning to soak through the fabric.

Her gaze slid over his bare, muscled torso, not missing the scrape across his right shoulder and the ugly purple color already starting to darken the skin.

"Damned armadillo," he cursed.

She met his scowl. "Armadillo?"

"Yeah." His scowl deepened. "I swerved to miss it and the bike went spinning out of control. Know what's the worst of the deal? It just lumbered on past me without a glance, off into the damned sagebrush."

"And left you in a mess, it seems."

"And the bike unridable," he added. "Don't happen to know a good mechanic around here, do you?"

Mariah's gaze swept over him. "Right now I think it's more important to get you seen to. Some of those cuts and scrapes look serious."

Luke didn't agree. He was a doctor—at least enough of one to know that the wounds were mostly superficial. But what he'd done for the last ten years of his life was not something he wanted to reveal to this woman. It would only bring on the inevitable questions, questions he didn't want to answer.

"Look, I'm fine," he said. "The only thing seriously damaged is my pride. No man wants to admit he was brought down by a miserable armadillo."

His answer didn't dissuade her from her concern, though it did prompt a smile, a smile that could pump a little daylight into the dark reaches of his heart—if he allowed it to.

He tried to forget the brightness in her smile, but it wasn't as easy to ignore her touch when her fingers brushed his shoulder softly, gently, probingly.

She knelt in front of him and examined the wound in his leg, loosening the makeshift dressing to make her own assessment of the damage. Her touch was as confident as any surgeon's—and damningly sensual. That last thought had him sucking in a breath.

She glanced up. "Sorry—does that hurt?"

There was innocence pooled in her green eyes, the kind that could make a man believe in the world again. But that would be a tall order for Luke.

"Would a macho guy like me admit it if it did?" he returned.

That brought another smile to her pretty lips, and for one dangerous moment he wanted to crush those lips with his own, feel them part for him, taste their sweetness and that all-fired innocence of hers. There was something so natural about her, nurturing, and a serenity he envied.

"Look—we've got to get you cleaned up," she said as she retied the dressing on his leg. "My truck is parked nearby. Sit still, and I'll go get it. We can load the cycle in the back."

He glanced at her slender body and decided the woman wouldn't be of much use in the loading department.

"Don't go anywhere," she said.

As if Luke had anyplace to go in this wilderness.

As if he had anyplace to go at all.

He leaned back against the tree and watched as she disappeared on down the road. He should have asked her how far she had to go to retrieve that truck of hers. A mile? Ten miles? Luke had the feeling distance didn't mean all that much to her, that she was well-accustomed to getting where she wanted to go—and under her own power.

He frowned at his now-useless bike and ran a hand over his jaw. How the hell had he gotten himself into this mess? But that wasn't something he wanted to think about.

It was more than one nuisance armadillo in the road.

It was why he was on this road in the first place, what had happened in the trauma unit that one tragic night—and his inability to live with himself because of it.

He wasn't sure how long he could keep on running from his pain—or if he could ever escape it. All he knew was that it had traveled with him every mile of his journey.

An unwanted companion on his ride to nowhere.

* * *

It didn't take Mariah long to retrieve the truck from where she'd parked it. But there was no time for that cooling splash in the stream she'd planned on—not today.

Luke needed her attention.

Already she was thinking ahead to what herbs she had on hand to treat his cuts and bruises. That was, if he held still for her simple remedies.

He probably preferred modern medicine. But it was a long drive to the nearest clinic. She hadn't wanted to tell him that. Or that it was an even longer drive to the nearest repair shop for his motorcycle.

The old truck started on the first try, which was some-thing of a minor miracle. Usually she had to coax it to life, promising the metal heap she wouldn't sell it to the first passerby.

Mariah patted the dashboard and smiled, then released the gear and turned the truck around, bouncing over the sagebrush toward the road—and Luke.

Visions of the man, minus his shirt, shimmered before her eyes. She hadn't been able to draw her gaze away from him, from the smattering of dark, golden hair that arrowed enticingly down to his waist and disap-peared beneath his low-slung jeans.

He was easily the most handsome man she'd ever seen. Not that she had seen that many handsome men— but growing up in the Hopi world, Mariah had learned to appreciate the beauty and form of nature.

And the man she'd left sitting under that spindly cot-tonwood tree was nature at its most perfect.

Her hands felt damp on the steering wheel, and her heart pounded way too fast. What was the matter with her? Luke was a patient, one who needed her attention. She should be concentrating on the man's injuries, not his tempting body.

The truck coughed and sputtered over the next rise, then Luke came into view. He stood as she neared, shielding his eyes against the sun to watch her approach.

She stopped and executed a turn, backing the truck up in front of the cycle so it would be easier for them to load.

"That thing's quite a relic," he said, standing back to take in the truck with a slow, sweeping glance.

"At least it runs," Mariah returned.

She lowered the tailgate with a rasp of metal, then dragged out a weather-beaten old board from the back end to use as a makeshift ramp.

"Look, you're not exactly the weighty help I need to load this baby into the back end," he said, running a critical eye over her smallish shape.

Mariah drew herself up taller. "That may be, but I don't see anyone else lining up to offer his services, do you?"

Luke cursed inventively and ran a hand through his hair. He hated being at anyone's mercy—especially a woman who heated his blood the way Mariah did.

He caught her soft scent, sweet and sun-drenched—like the flowers she collected in her basket. Her red blouse dipped just low enough at the neck to reveal the slightest hint of her delectable breasts beneath.

Her arms were bronzed by the sun, slender, capable; just not capable of raising his bike to the bed of her truck, though he had no doubt that she would try.

He had the feeling that she was accomplished at many things, that she had to be. Perhaps she was alone in the world, with no one to share the emotional and physical load she carried—or did she prefer to carry it all herself?

She made him curious, though he had no right to be anything of the sort. This was only a chance meeting of two people in time, one moment of accident that had brought them together.

He longed to feed his soul with her warmth, something he denied himself because of his failure that night in the trauma unit.

The night he couldn't work his medical magic.

The night he failed to save his son.

Chapter Two

"This is Sunrise," Mariah said as they passed through the tiny town of only a few businesses.

A small grocery store, an old tavern, a pizza place and a post office surrounded the small center plaza. Several square-shaped houses were scattered around the town's outskirts. And up on the hill beyond sat the church with its old bell tower, the bell long-since missing.

"You live in town?" he asked.

She glanced over at him, his injured leg stretched out in front of him as best he could in the cramped cab of her truck. She needed to take care of that leg wound. It had to be painful—despite his insistence to the contrary.

The man pretended toughness—and Mariah suspected he wasn't about to admit to simple weaknesses like cuts and scrapes and bruises.

"I live a short distance beyond. It's not far," she said as the truck rumbled past the town's environs.

Callie would be waiting for her at home. And Una would have supper started. She always did when Mariah was away gathering her herbs and roots.

Both would be surprised she was bringing home a guest of sorts.

A few miles ahead she made a turn, the truck creaking and groaning as if it were an old woman getting out of a rocker after a long afternoon nap.

She passed Una's small frame-and-stucco house. Her own was just past it, not much larger size-wise, but with a wide porch that Mariah loved. She often sat out there at the end of her day, listening to the night sounds, enjoying the solitude—and thinking of the day to come.

"Here we are," she said, as she pulled into the long driveway and parked a short distance from the house.

Luke surveyed his surroundings. The house was small, but it exuded a warmth that was very much Mariah. Maybe it was the big front porch, or perhaps the soft, fluttery white curtains at the windows or the well-tended garden at the side, but he liked it. Liked its soft cream color, its peace and simplicity.

He opened the truck door and swung his injured leg out. If it hadn't been for his little mishap back on the road, he'd have been halfway to Phoenix by now. Not that he was on any schedule.

Not since he'd left his life fifteen-hundred miles behind.

"Mommy! Mommy!"

Luke glanced up to see a little girl of about six, maybe seven, tripping toward them. The first thing he noticed was her beauty—dark silken hair, like her mother's, and the same vibrant green eyes.

The brightness in her face, her smile, eclipsed the other thing he noticed—sturdy braces on her thin, coltish legs, braces that at the moment weren't impeding her progress much.

Mariah came around the side of the truck and swept the child up in her arms. "Callie, this is Luke Phillips," she said.

"Hi, Luke Phillips," she answered, using his whole name, much the same way her mother had earlier.

Luke liked the sound of it. He also liked the smile on Mariah's face, the one that matched her daughter's.

Friendliness was a way of life out here, it seemed, and it was Luke's good fortune that it was. Otherwise he'd be sitting back there along the road with nothing but cactus for company.

The little girl was like a bright ray of sunshine after a long, dark day, he thought, and stuck out his hand. She accepted it shyly, her grasp light, innocent, her hand tiny in his.

Luke recognized instantly that this was a child who'd experienced pain, but there was no sign of it in her sweet smile, or the confident raise of her chin—as if she, like her mother, wasn't afraid to take on the world at large.

"Hi, Callie," he returned.

She glanced down at the shirt tied around his thigh, then at the scrapes and bruises on his shoulder and jaw. "You got hurt," she said. "Is my mommy gonna fix you up?"

He swept his gaze from Callie to Mariah. Luke wasn't exactly used to being on the receiving end of medicine, but he suspected Mariah knew how to dispense treatment, along with a little peace, a peace a man could get used to—if he allowed it.

"I am," Mariah answered her daughter. "Luke had a little…*accident.* He had to swerve to miss an armadillo with his motorcycle."

That made the little girl giggle. At the moment Luke didn't see much humor in the incident—but he allowed a hint of a smile to break through anyway.

"Come on inside and meet Una," Mariah urged as she set her daughter down, cautious until Callie was steady on her braces.

"Who is Una?" he asked.

"My neighbor. And friend. She watches Callie for me when I need her. And if I know Una, she has a pot of her Southwest stew simmering on the stove."

"No, Mommy—she made chili," Callie told her. "Do you like chili?" she asked Luke.

"It so happens I love chili," he answered the little girl. She smiled.

"First we clean your war wounds," Mariah announced.

Luke's leg was beginning to stiffen up on him. And it hurt like the devil. But he didn't intend to admit *that* to Mariah. "I'm okay," he said.

She gave him a look that said she didn't believe that for a moment, then started toward the house. Callie bounded ahead of them, somehow managing gracefully on her braces.

"She's a beautiful child," Luke said.

Mariah smiled. Mother-pride shone in her eyes— but it didn't quite hide that small shadow of sadness Luke caught in their sea-green depths.

"Callie's a delight," she said. "My bright joy. I—I just wish things could be…different for her," she said softly.

Luke knew she meant the stiff braces Callie wore. His professional guess would be that the child had a form of juvenile rheumatoid arthritis.

He'd seen the disease in its cruel form during his pediatric work in med school. He knew its effects. But he didn't know how to offer comfort any more than he knew how to find it for himself.

They found Una in the kitchen. Callie had already informed her they were having a guest for supper tonight.

"Help me set another place at the table," Una told the child, then she turned and gave Luke a once-over. "Father Sky above! You look like you got skinned by a bear."

Luke grimaced. "I'm afraid it wasn't anything quite that fierce, ma'am."

Mariah hid a grin, but she didn't elaborate on his scrapes and bruises—or how he'd come by them.

"A little sunflower and a sprinkle of ground willow bark—that ought to fix him up." Una gave her prescriptive advice with a brisk nod to Mariah.

It was exactly what Mariah had in mind for her patient—providing the man would sit still for it.

She wasn't sure he would.

"Why don't you boil some water," she told Una, "while I get this man stripped."

Luke's eyes widened in surprise for a quick moment, then a very male frown took its place on his face. "It's only a few scratches. I can look after them myself."

"The injury to your thigh needs treatment—and so does your shoulder. If you have a problem with that, you can complain about it later." She motioned him toward a small room off the kitchen. Finding a large blue towel in the cabinet, she pulled it down and handed it to him. "I'll go help Una with that hot water. You get out of those jeans," she told him.

Luke grumbled under his breath as she left the room, but he undid the shirt he'd tied around his leg as a make-shift compress. Beneath it the gash didn't look too bad, he decided. It wasn't deep enough to need suturing. Just bothersome enough to make riding out of here uncomfortable. That was, if he could even find someplace to repair his cycle.

Luke knew one armadillo with a price on its head.

He'd just finished sliding off his jeans when he heard Mariah return.

"Are you decent?" she called through the closed door.

Luke frowned. "As decent as I can get wearing damned little," he answered, dragging the towel around him, and wishing it had a little extra yardage.

Mariah kept her eyes averted as she entered the room, wishing there was some other way to do this. And that her patient wasn't so overwhelming. Both dressed or in the altogether.

Luke Phillips had more male appeal than the laws of nature should allow, an innate masculinity she was having a difficult time dealing with at the moment.

Her hormones bucked, but she tamped down her reaction to the man and set the bowl of steaming water on the small worktable in front of her, then motioned Luke to a chair.

She would get through this somehow, hopefully with her wanton hormones intact.

"Una sent you a little firewater, in lieu of a bullet to

bite on," she said, drawing a pint-size bottle of whiskey from the back pocket of her jeans.

That produced a wide-eyed glance from Luke, followed by a slow smile—a smile that was as potent as the rest of him beneath that blue towel.

"You expect the surgery to be that bad, Doc?"

He was teasing her. Mariah swallowed hard and tried to remain calm, focusing her gaze on his wounds instead of his broad chest and equally broad shoulders, every muscle firm and sleek and tanned. The man was too good-looking for comfort.

Her comfort.

Awareness clawed at her nerves here in the close confines of the room. She tried to picture him fully clothed instead of in that precarious blue towel.

But it did little for her senses.

His broad shoulders would fill out a shirt to perfection—or a suit. Did he wear a tux back where he came from—perhaps for a special event?

Or a date?

That thought flashed into her mind and she tamped down her reaction, trying to focus on the task at hand.

"I'll try to be gentle," she said.

His body heat radiated to her in the small room. He smelled of fresh air and sunshine and forbidden stranger. And it was having a decided effect on her.

Luke watched Mariah work, sprinkling something into the water he supposed was that ground willow bark Una had talked about, then dipped a soft, white washcloth into the mixture. But he hadn't been ready for her touch as she cleansed the gash on his thigh.

Her hands were gentle, yet sure—and damningly

sensual. He struggled with the effect they had on his body, and decided a little of Una's firewater might be in order after all.

Not to dull the pain in his leg—but to numb his suddenly threatening testosterone.

"Damn," he cursed, then sucked in a breath and reached for the bottle of whiskey.

"Sorry, does this hurt?"

He was in a world of hurt—and not sure he'd survive. Her touch was driving him wild. "I think that's good enough," he ground out. "Why don't you work on my shoulder for a while?"

"Your shoul—oh!"

The light dawned in her pretty green eyes and a heated blush climbed her neck and spread across her cheeks before she glanced away, unable to meet his gaze.

"I'll just rinse the cloth and…and…"

He put a hand on her arm, then thought better of it and drew it away. "It's okay, Mariah. I'm, uh, just on a rather short fuse right now."

Her reply was a deeper blush, and Luke took a long swallow of whiskey.

"Tell me about Callie," he said as she immersed her cloth in the hot mixture again. He needed to get his mind off the tempting woman beside him, and conversation was the best way he knew to deal with the situation. Besides, he wanted to know more about her, about Callie, about their life out here in the middle of nowhere. "The plants you gathered…they're for your daughter, aren't they?"

Mariah dabbed the herbal solution onto Luke's shoulder wound. She'd been so engrossed in her work, cleansing the injury on his thigh, that she hadn't realized she'd been…*affecting* him. It seemed that this awareness was a problem on both their parts.

Her hands shook at the merest brush of his skin and her heart beat heavily. How long had it been since she'd been this close to a gorgeous male? Never, she admitted. At least not one as gorgeous as Luke.

Will had been good-looking, she supposed. At least she'd once thought so—then she'd seen the ugliness beneath the surface.

There'd been no man in her life since Will had left, which suited Mariah just fine. She'd been sorely hurt by his defection, hurt that he could care so little about his daughter.

Callie was what was important to her now.

She always would be.

"Yes," she said. "The herbs are for Callie—for her arthritis, at least most of them are. Una taught me their uses, when the doctor's medicine failed to help."

Luke seemed to understand about Callie. He hadn't shown the slightest surprise when she'd come bounding toward them on her cumbersome braces. Instead he'd seen her beauty and the sun in her smile.

"Callie's had conventional treatment, then?"

She nodded at his question. Mariah had had her daughter to the best doctors in Phoenix, spending the last pittance of money she had on their treatments, the newest medicines.

"Nothing seemed to work for her," she said. "At least, not to any degree. It was a long trip to Phoenix for care, and the ride often left Callie worse because of it. Then Una told me of the healing power in the plants and herbs that grow around here. Callie seems to thrive on them."

"And perhaps a little on her mother's love?"

Mariah gave him a quick glance and saw a pensive look on his face, the shadow of something in his eyes. Luke was a man who was hurting—and not from the wounds she could see, the wounds he'd received in that tumble from his bike, the wounds she hoped her herbs would heal.

It was the other wound, the one she could only sense, the one that claimed his soul, his spirit, that she wasn't sure she could do anything about. She suspected that wound ran deep. But whatever his torment was, it was none of her business.

At least none that he would share with her.

"Yes," she said softly. "Callie's very special to me."

Luke wondered what it would be like to be someone special in Mariah's life. He suspected she loved with a fervor, an honesty, a completeness. And when she gave herself to that love, she'd never take it back.

Mariah was a nurturer. She found comfort in the very world around her. She took it from the earth and gave it to others. To her daughter. And even to Luke.

A total stranger.

He hoped this medicine of hers worked damned fast—because Mariah could make a man want to stick around, seek a little of that comfort she dispensed.

Finally finishing with his shoulder, she reached to cleanse the scrape along his jawline. Her touch was feather-soft, soothing.

"I'm afraid you're not going to feel like shaving anytime soon," she said, cleansing his jaw and applying some cool ointment to it, something that smelled faintly of lavender.

He knew she was right about the shaving. Maybe he'd grow a serious beard—and he wondered if Mariah would like the rasp of it when he kissed her.

Before Luke let that thought play itself out further in his mind he reached up and grasped her hand. Her touch was driving him wild, her closeness a temptation he wasn't sure he could resist, at least not for long.

"Sorry, I didn't mean to hurt—"

"You didn't hurt me," he said. But neither could he let her touch him. The feel of her hands, no matter how purposeful, how innocent, was impossible for him to ignore. "I'm fine, Mariah. You've done enough."

She fixed him with a determined gaze and a stern lift of her chin. "That leg wound needs a dressing."

He groaned low in his throat, and was certain his soul was damned—damned by this bewitching female who was intent on helping him.

It was just his rotten luck to find a *perfectionist* for a healer.

"This will only take a minute," she insisted. "It won't hurt a bit. You'll see."

Easy for her to say, Luke thought, as he steeled himself against her touch.

Her hands were brisk, her movements sure and smooth. The woman was grace and loveliness, all rolled into an all-too-tempting package.

He gritted his teeth as her fingers applied the gauze, pressing it against the raw gash. Every nerve ending jumped to attention at the lightest touch of her silky fingers.

His wayward hormones must be there, too, he decided, because they sang with raw need at her closeness, her flowery scent, her soft, feminine heat.

"There—that should do it," she said, applying the last strip of tape and standing back to admire her handiwork.

Her cheeks glowed, her eyes big and green in the play of light in the room. A smile brushed her sweet lips—and Luke knew he'd never seen a more beautiful woman.

"Thank you," he told her, though he suspected she didn't need to hear it.

It was simply her nature to help—whether it be man, woman or child. Mariah was a healer—as much as any doctor he knew. It flowed from her like a life force, a gift Luke had to envy.

And admire.

"I think Una probably has that chili ready—if you're hungry," she said, then began gathering up her medical supplies with skillful efficiency.

"I'm starved," he admitted. "Then I need to find someplace to stay for the night. Is there a motel in Sunrise?"

"Sorry, no, there isn't. There's no place close. It's not much, but there's a small cabin out back. Callie likes to use it as her playhouse, but you're welcome to it, if you like. It's clean, and I can bring you some fresh linens. You'd be comfortable."

Luke didn't doubt that. But how much more of her hospitality could he let himself accept?

He started to refuse and then remembered he had no transportation. And he couldn't ask her to drive him miles to the nearest hotel.

She had Callie to consider.

He'd have to take her up on her offer, then find a way to repay her for her kindness. As soon as his cycle was operational again, he'd be on his way.

It was all he could do under the circumstances.

"I accept," he said. "At least for tonight."

Tomorrow he'd assess his circumstances and come up with an alternative plan, providing an alternative existed out here—miles from anywhere.

A short time later they were gathered around the kitchen table, enjoying Una's chili and warm corn bread. Mariah noticed that the beleaguered place mats were gone, replaced by her one good linen tablecloth. Una had obviously deemed this man deserving of special status.

Callie had chosen to sit next to Luke, and she chattered away to him like a magpie. Her daughter was more exuberant than usual tonight.

And Mariah had no doubt it was prompted by their guest.

If Sunrise had a disadvantage it was in its sameness. Very little new or different made its way here. So Luke Phillips at tonight's dinner table was an event on par with Christmas.

Mariah stole a quick glance at him. He'd donned a fresh shirt pulled from one of his saddlebags, a white knit polo that hugged his muscled chest and showed off his tan to perfection.

He'd borrowed her kitchen shears and fashioned his torn jeans into a pair of cutoffs. They, too, hugged him in dangerous places.

He turned to glance at her, and she hoped he hadn't

caught her ogling. His face bore an uncertain expression, and she wondered what he was thinking.

She sensed he was a man who concealed his emotions, not sharing them easily with others. It was something Mariah could understand. She shared herself only with a few people she knew and trusted.

She glanced at Luke's empty bowl. "Would you care for more chili?" she asked.

He smiled and patted his flat stomach. "Thanks, but no. I'm definitely full." He turned to Una seated at the other end of the table. "That was delicious, ma'am. I don't think I've ever tasted any better."

Una let a rare smile slip, obviously pleased with the compliment.

Was she, too, caught up in Luke's charm?

There were probably few females who could resist a man as compelling as Luke Phillips, she decided.

Mariah didn't know where he'd been headed on that big Harley of his, but he'd no doubt leave a trail of broken hearts along the way. And perhaps where he'd come from, as well.

Was he married? There was no ring on his left hand, no lighter mark where one had been on his tanned skin.

Did he have children?

He seemed so capable, so at ease around Callie.

What was his life? she wondered. And what was the cause of the pain she saw in his storm-blue eyes? She admitted she was curious, though she had no right to be.

All she'd done was rescue him in the desert and treat his wounds.

As soon as he had transportation again, he'd be leaving.

She stood and began to gather up the supper dishes.

"You've done enough for one day, Una. I'll clean up in here."

"I'll help," Luke offered.

"Good," Una said. "I promised Callie a story before I go home."

The pair retreated to the front porch swing, Callie's favorite spot for hearing Una's Hopi tales, leaving Mariah alone with Luke in the big kitchen that suddenly seemed a whole lot smaller.

Chapter Three

With both of them working together it didn't take long to finish the dishes. Luke enjoyed the task—or maybe it was just being alone with Mariah.

He couldn't remember having been stuck with KP duty growing up. Nor could he remember having helped his wife, Sylvie, during their ill-fated marriage. He'd been the golden doctor then—slated to take his place in the hierarchy of the hospital where his father and grandfather had practiced before him.

Luke had never considered himself special—he'd just been treated like he was. It had been a given that he would do great things.

He hadn't helped Sylvie raise their son, Dane, either. At least not as much as he should have. He'd been at the hospital night and day, doing what he loved. Doing what was important. All other work he'd relegated to Sylvie.

No doubt the reason she'd left him for someone else.

He wished he could go back, do things differently, be a real father to his son. But life didn't work that way. Life wouldn't let a man turn back the clock.

Life took—and didn't give back.

One failed marriage, his failure as a father—and as a doctor who couldn't save his son—had taken its toll on Luke's ability to believe the world could be a happy place.

Yet tonight he'd glimpsed something akin to that in this small family that had included him in their life however briefly. Tonight he'd been able to forget, just a little.

Tossing the dish towel onto the countertop, he turned to Mariah. "Consider that payment for tonight's dinner. Now, about your medical fee…"

Mariah gave a soft laugh, a sensual sound that could curl a man's toes. "You don't owe me anything," she said. "But I do think you need to get off that leg for a while."

"I was thinking more like a short walk to loosen it up."

"Elevating your leg is sound medical advice," she said, arms folded resolutely over her chest.

"I'd rather take that walk. Join me?" he asked.

He hoped she would say yes. He wanted to be with her. He liked her, liked this little family—and he felt like walking, absorbing the night and its dark peace.

She seemed to hesitate. "I—I need to get Callie tucked into bed."

Of course, he thought. Callie would require an early bedtime. Proper rest would be an important part of treatment for a child with this disease, Luke knew. And Mariah would be a stickler for what was best for her daughter.

"I understand," he said.

"If you want to wait, I could go in a little while," she added, and Luke's head came up.

He read something indefinable in her eyes, and suspected she didn't often take time for herself. Time away from Callie. She had her priorities and they were in the right place.

Her daughter came first.

He wished now that he'd put Dane ahead of other things in his life. Why had his medical career, the hospital, seemed so damned important, anyway? He'd have made it to the top—it just would have taken him a little longer.

And in the end, none of it had mattered.

"I can wait," he answered. "I'll even prop up my leg."

She smiled at that, then turned to leave. "I won't be long."

Luke nodded. "Take your time."

Mariah's living room was warm and inviting. The walls were a soft cream, uncluttered by pictures or other bric-a-brac. There was an old stone fireplace at one end for cool evenings, with two blue overstuffed chairs flanking it, a red-plaid sofa facing it.

Luke decided on one of the chairs and pulled up a small footstool to prop his leg on. The damned thing had begun to throb again. So had his shoulder.

Not that he intended to let Mariah know that.

On the table beside him was a picture of her with Callie, a soft mother-daughter pose that stirred him. Mariah's dark hair was worn loose, cascading over her shoulder, as she gazed down at a laughing Callie.

Visions of the woman treating his wounds, the

memory of her sensual touch, would torment him half the night, he was certain. He was equally certain he needed to keep a tight rein on his emotions. Mariah was tempting, a beautiful woman, one who'd be hard to resist for long.

He'd better just hope he could put his Harley in working order again—and fast. He was in no position to involve himself with this small family, with Mariah. He had nothing to offer her.

He had nothing to offer anyone.

His life was in sorry shape and going nowhere. He no longer knew up from down, right from left. He'd spun out of control after Dane's death, hating himself, hating medicine, hating life itself.

From the other room he could hear Mariah's lilting voice, sometimes Callie's sweet laugh. The sound of his son's laughter echoed through his memory—laughter Luke would never hear again.

The accident had happened on his son's eighth birthday. The car had come racing around the corner and struck him, leaving his small battered body for Luke to salvage. He closed his eyes against the damning memories.

Don't think about it, he cautioned himself.

Don't think about anything.

It seemed a long while later when Mariah returned to the living room, but he knew it hadn't been. She glanced at his leg, propped on the footstool, and offered that soft smile of hers.

"Are you sure you want that walk? You look like you're right where you should be—resting that leg."

Luke didn't need rest. He needed to be moving. If he

couldn't roar off down the highway on his Harley, he'd pace the yard, the road, walk for miles, and then some. He wanted—needed—to escape his pain, the memories. How far would he need to ride to put his life behind him?

"Yeah, I want that walk," he said.

He pushed to his feet, then saw the small frown of worry that had edged itself between her brows. Mariah was concerned about him, concerned about his injuries—but she needn't be. He was fine. He'd *be* fine. Luke was tough—just not tough enough to deal with one little boy's death.

He strode toward the front door, careful not to show signs of pain, careful not to limp on his leg that had stiffened up on him.

Outside, the night was cool. A breeze tugged at his senses. A perfect counterpoint to the hot, dusty day. For a moment he found himself relaxing, letting go.

Mariah fell into step beside him. Her soft scent wafted over him, and the night tortured him with the temptation to reach for her, to tuck her hand in his, to press her to him and taste her lips that glistened so softly in the moonlight. Jamming his hands into the pockets of his cutoffs, he drew in a deep breath of air.

Dangerous thoughts, he knew.

But he didn't know how to rid himself of them.

They reached the small copse of trees at the back of Mariah's property. A stream ran through here, with cool, clear water burbling and purling over the flat stones on its way to lower ground.

"This is my favorite place. I like to come here," she said. "It's always refreshing on a hot afternoon."

And tempting at night with the moonlight slanting

through the trees, Luke thought. Mariah's eyes were luminescent, her lips soft and smooth, and he fought back the urge to taste them.

Just once.

He reached down and plucked a small stone from the streambed, turning it over and over in his hand. "I can see why it's your favorite spot," he said. "It's beautiful here."

She smiled, apparently pleased he liked it, too.

"Tell me about yourself, Mariah."

She took a step or two away, then sat down on the grassy bank. Her hair gleamed dark in the moonlight; her skin shimmered like warm bronze.

And her mouth...

Her mouth was made for kissing.

He tore his gaze away and tossed the stone back into the stream, counting the ripples that ebbed away.

"What do you want to know?"

Luke heard her small voice as if it were coming from a distance. "Have you always lived here?"

She plucked a blade of grass and ran it through her fingers, absorbing its damp coolness. "I grew up nearby," she answered. "On the Reservation. The *Rez*, as it's affectionately called. Then two years ago Callie and I moved here."

When Will had left them. She'd had very little money and a lot of doctor bills. The house had sat empty for years. Ever since her grandfather's death.

It had been in sorry shape when they'd moved in, but still it had been a godsend to Mariah. She'd fixed it up little by little and she was proud of what she had accomplished.

Will's leaving, and her subsequent divorce from him six months later, had been hard on Callie. It had been hard on her, as well. But she and Callie had forged a new life for themselves, and it was a good life, a happy one.

"What about you?" she asked. "Where are you from?"

Her question seemed to cause him pain. His eyes darkened and he glanced aside. "A long way from here—Chicago."

Chicago might as well be a foreign country to Mariah. She'd never been farther away than Phoenix. She wondered about Luke's life there, tried to picture him with a wife, a family.

Did he have a wife?

A lover?

Was she beautiful?

"Sunrise is a far cry from where you're from," she said. "Where are you headed on that big bike of yours?"

And who's missing you at home? she wanted to add.

Luke was handsome. The women in Chicago would have to be blind not to find him so. She was certain someone had staked a claim to him by now.

He gave a small shrug of his broad shoulders. "As of this afternoon, I'm not headed anywhere, it seems. Not until my bike is operational again."

"And then?" she probed.

"West."

"That takes in a lot of territory. Anything more specific?"

He frowned. "Are you always this inquisitive?"

"Only about stray men I rescue from the desert," she quipped back, which made him smile.

The first smile she'd seen on him in a while.

It was devastatingly seductive, and she forced herself to picture a wife waiting for him back in Chicago. And maybe a passel of kids. *Little* kids.

And one on the way.

But it didn't gel. No matter how hard she tried, she couldn't place Luke in a domestic scene.

"Are you married?"

Her words had tumbled out—and she felt instantly foolish for them.

His smile broadened. "I was right about that inquisitiveness of yours. But no, I'm not married."

She didn't want to admit to herself that she was pleased. Secretly. Didn't want to admit that she found the man intriguing. That he could make her pulse pound with very little provocation.

She didn't need to fall for men who rode through town on motorcycles, stopping only long enough to tempt her heart. She'd vowed never to entangle herself with anyone who would leave again, who wouldn't stick around and be a real husband, who wouldn't be a father to Callie with all her special needs.

She didn't want Callie hurt again.

Or herself—by hoping for too much.

"I-I'm sorry, I shouldn't have asked that," she murmured.

"No harm done."

He held her gaze prisoner a little longer than he should have, and Mariah couldn't tear her own away. "Maybe I should get back," she said finally. "I hate to be away too long, in case Callie wakes up."

He helped her to her feet, and his touch sent a shiver

through her, one she knew had nothing to do with the cool night air. His gaze whispered over her lips, and she could almost taste his kiss.

In the space of one restless moment her need meshed with his and she thought he was going to kiss her, but instead he only reached out a hand and brushed her cheek.

"You're right, we'd better be getting back," he said.

Was there a hint of regret in his words?

Or had she imagined it?

Whichever, the moment had passed, and Mariah didn't know whether to be disappointed or relieved. What she felt was a strange mixture of both.

She'd never thought of herself as a needy woman. Or a lonely one. She had Callie. Her daughter was her life. She was happy. Her days were full and filled. So why could this man tempt her so easily in the moonlight?

She tried to shrug away the question as she walked, careful to keep a comfortable distance from him— though she wasn't sure what that distance might be.

"The cabin is over there, just beyond the rise," she said. "Come on, I'll show it to you."

Luke followed her across the property toward the small rough-hewn structure barely visible in the moonlight.

"It isn't much, like I said. I hope you don't mind roughing it a little."

"I'm sure it'll beat hard ground with a cactus for a pillow. I didn't see much else out there on that road I was on."

She turned and smiled at him. The softest, sweetest smile Luke could recall ever seeing on a woman.

"True enough," she said softly.

He'd found her so damned appealing back there in the cool grass, the moonlight slanting across her face, her sultry lips.

He wasn't sure why he didn't act on the moment, seize the chance to kiss her, taste the sweetness he knew he'd find on her lips.

He tried to shove that thought aside. It could only bring them both trouble. Mariah had a daughter. She wasn't someone interested in a brief fling. Though he wasn't at all sure any interlude with her could be brief.

The woman would be damned hard to walk away from when the time came to do so. He'd do well to keep that realization in mind the next time temptation hit him.

"This is it," Mariah said as they reached the cabin. "It's probably not what you're used to back in civilization."

She drew a lantern from its nail on the wall, found a match and lit the wick. Flickering light flooded the little room and Luke took a look around.

A small cot was pushed against one wall. There was also a chair—a little lumpy in the seat cushion, but usable—and a well-scarred coffee table.

A few toys and a rag doll with one eye missing were scattered about, and he remembered Mariah telling him Callie liked to use the cabin as her playhouse.

He picked up the doll and grinned at its one-eyed countenance, then set it aside. He remembered Dane's toys had always been scattered about, remembered how he'd hated it when he tripped over them. He wished now he could take back his annoyance over something so minor. But it was too late...

"The place is fine," he said. "I hope Callie won't mind my borrowing it for a while."

She gave him a soft smile. "Callie won't mind. Besides, I think she's quite taken with you."

"And what about her mother?"

"Her mother won't mind, either," she answered, unaware that wasn't the question he'd asked her.

"That wasn't what I meant," he said, taking a step closer. He reached out a hand and softly traced the margins of the blush that had risen to her cheeks. Her skin beneath his touch was silken. Her eyes were wide and filled with want. Or was it a trick of the flickering lantern light? "I wondered if Callie's mother was taken, too, just a little."

Her blush deepened. He could feel its heat beneath his fingertips. Mariah was warm and vibrant—and everything he *shouldn't* want in a woman. He was a man on the move. To where, he didn't know, didn't know if he'd ever get there, if he'd ever be whole again. One pretty woman with hopes and dreams—and needs— was a luxury he couldn't afford.

Not now, maybe never.

"I should go and find you some linens," she said quietly, her voice sounding as if it came from someplace far away.

She wasn't unaffected by him—any more than he was by her. But, somehow, that knowledge didn't make Luke feel any better about himself.

When Mariah returned with fresh sheets and towels for him, Luke was out front of the tiny cabin, studying the stars. Strange how he'd never noticed them back in Chicago. Or the moon. He could use the peace this place offered.

At least for a little while.

"Here are the linens," she said. "I'll just go and lay them on the cot."

Luke watched her go. He had no right to want her. He was hurting, and Mariah offered peace, if only a temporary peace. But he had nothing to offer her in return.

She deserved a man who could pluck down the moon for her, those cool, glittery stars. A man who could give her some of himself.

"Will you be comfortable for the night?" she asked, stepping out the cabin's front door.

Comfortable? More than he had been on the seat of a motorcycle. More than he'd been the last six months— since his son's death. "I'll be fine," he answered, hating the ragged sound to his voice.

"If you need anything, just let me know."

"I won't need anything."

She stepped off the porch slowly, a little unsurely. "I'll be getting back then," she said and started to leave.

Luke stopped her.

"Mariah?"

She turned softly to gaze at him, and Luke knew he was lost, lost in those luminous green eyes, that prettily shaped mouth, her haunting femininity.

He'd only wanted to thank her for what she'd done, but she stood so close he could touch her, stroke her hair, smooth back the few rebellious strands that escaped her braid.

"Thank you," he managed to get out. "For…everything."

She smiled softly, and it was his undoing.

He brushed the back of his fingers along her cheek, then her lower lip, tracing its silken curve. She didn't draw away, only gazed up at him with her own soft need.

His resolve melted completely. He had to taste her lips,

just once. He leaned down and brushed them lightly with his own, finding something that surely had to be heaven.

His tongue traced them slowly, outlining their shape, memorizing it for the long, lonely night ahead of him. Still she didn't pull away, and he tasted deeper, wanting what he shouldn't have.

She kissed him back, thoroughly, sending his soul into the darker regions of hell. Her mouth was sweet and sinful, her breasts soft and full as they pushed gently against him. Mariah was delight and innocence, peace and treasure, all in one dangerous package.

She gave a slow sigh, then drew away. She was trembling and wouldn't meet his gaze. "I—I…we shouldn't…"

"I know," he said, agreeing totally. He didn't dare touch her again. "I'm sorry, Mariah."

Her troubled eyes flickered and she met his gaze for one eternal moment, then she turned and fled, back up the path to the house.

Consigning him to a night of tortured want.

What had she done?

Mariah hurried along the path to the house, determined to escape inside and bar the door. Not to keep Luke out, but herself in. Safely in. She had just thrown herself at the man.

A perfect stranger.

Hadn't she gotten herself in trouble just this way before, with Will? Except that at least Will hadn't been a stranger. Will had been the first boy she'd known who lived off the Rez. And that had seemed exciting.

She'd seen him often, thought him special, older,

though a little wild. She'd liked the wild part. He'd invited her to a party and she had gone. There'd been beer and the music was loud and electrifying; Mariah had felt she'd finally escaped the Rez. She could do what she wanted.

The party had been in an old, abandoned adobe out in the desert. Her new friends, Will's friends, used the place to party, drink beer, get high on marijuana and sometimes peyote. She'd been afraid of the drinking and drugs, and told Will she'd thought they were going to dance.

Mariah loved to dance; she'd wanted to dance with Will. But he insisted she smoke the marijuana, then he'd dance with her. The stuff had made her nauseous, light-headed, but she'd wanted to fit in, wanted Will to *like* her. She'd gone along that night with anything Will had wanted—and her life had changed.

But Mariah was no longer a teenager. And that kiss she'd just shared with Luke had been the kiss of a man, not a young, still-wet-behind-the-ears boy.

And that made it twice as dangerous.

She'd felt Luke's need, and her own, as if lightning had struck, searing her to the spot and her body to his. She could still feel the smoldering kiss, his mouth enticing, hauntingly sensual. She'd felt comfort in his arms, as if sheltered for the moment from all things bad.

Something she certainly had never felt with Will.

But Luke was temporary, fleeting. He'd be leaving as soon as his motorcycle was repaired, and her life would once again go back to the routine she was used to.

She needed to find her composure that had scattered like the wind with that kiss. She needed to find her sanity, too. She could not afford to lose herself around a man like Luke, a man who was headed out as soon as he could, a man with a painful past she shouldn't be curious about. A man who didn't belong here, didn't understand this way of life.

Her life.

She leaned her shoulder against the door frame, willing the calm back into her body, forcing her mind to return to reality.

She didn't know how long she'd stood there, how many minutes had passed, how many waves of temptation washed over her before she finally pushed away and embraced the reality of her world again.

A noisy raven had awakened Luke with its annoying call. It had been 3:35 the last time he'd pressed the lighted dial of his watch to note the time, and now it was 5:30—which meant he'd had only a couple hours of sleep.

And a fitful sleep at that.

Thoughts of Mariah had kept him tossing and turning, hoping for even the briefest respite from his troubled thoughts and perfect recall of her body.

Just holding her, touching her, had been madness, awakening every hormone he had, and weakening his defenses. He'd tasted those lips and was certain heaven couldn't be any sweeter.

His hands had traced the column of her spine, feeling its curve, its strength and power. Mariah was a woman tough enough to take on whatever came her way, yet malleable to the needs of others, to bend down and help a child.

Or to meld against him.

He'd wanted to go on holding her, kissing her, but he knew the danger in that. He couldn't take from her goodness, no matter how badly he wanted to.

He stared at the rough-planked ceiling over his bed, knowing sleep was hopeless now. The beginning shadows of daylight were already seeping into the cabin, through the tiny windows, through the chinks between the half logs that made up the cabin's walls.

And then there was the raven.

The damn pesky bird had to be sitting on the pitch of the roof directly over his head, caterwauling like mad. He thought he remembered that the feathered creatures were considered sacred or something in this part of the country—and that it was bad luck to harm one of them.

But Luke had had enough.

If the bird didn't stop with the crowing shrieks, reverberating through his brain like a fire bell on steroids, he might just forget about that sacredness and bad luck.

Especially if it gave him a few more minutes of shut-eye.

Silence. There were three whole minutes of blessed silence. Luke hollowed out a spot for his head on the pillow and closed his eyes, hoping the noisy raven had developed a bad case of laryngitis.

Sleep. He needed sleep. He closed his eyes and attempted to shut down his mind, as well, shut out the crazy bird, shut out his haunting thoughts of Mariah and the glory of her kiss, her slender body pressed so innocently against his.

He rolled onto his stomach, hoping for even ten minutes of rest. The cot, though small, was amazingly comfortable, and the sheets Mariah had brought him carried her mesmerizing scent.

Luke had barely been able to make up the bed last night with the soft scent teasing at him, reminding him of her freshness, of the sunshine that seemed to surround her and her little corner of the world.

Sleep, Luke thought. Then he'd get up and start in on his cycle. Once it was repaired he'd be on his way again.

And Mariah's kiss would be only a fond memory.

Chapter Four

Mariah awoke with a start. And not to the sound of the annoying raven's call that usually dragged her from sleep. This was different. This was the clang of metal against metal.

She hopped out of bed, and the covers she wasn't quite ready to abandon, and drew aside the lace curtain. The pink, early morning light of day danced through the window and into the room, catching on everything. Mariah ignored it in favor of finding out what the noise was all about. She didn't want it to wake Callie.

The sunlight glinted off Luke's bike and the man who stood staring at the pieces he'd dismantled. Her heart bumped at the sight of him—and she instantly remembered his kiss last night, the forbidden way it had tasted.

Luke had dragged dangerous needs to the surface,

stirring longings in her she thought she'd buried long ago. He had the power to make her vulnerable, make her lose all good sense—and that was something she'd promised herself no man would do to her again.

She had responsibilities, a daughter to look after. She couldn't afford to let *any* man foolishly turn her head—or hurt her, the way Will had done.

She focused her thoughts and her gaze on the cycle part Luke was inspecting. The thing didn't look salvageable to her, but he must believe he could force it into some kind of workable shape.

She dropped the curtain back into place, then hurriedly dressed in fresh-washed jeans and a loose denim shirt. She gave her hair a slight consideration in the bedroom mirror and declared it passable after some finger-combing to straighten out the tangles. She didn't have time right now for her usual braid.

She went to Callie's room and peeked in at her daughter. She was asleep, her dark hair spilled across the pillow. Fortunately the noise hadn't awakened her.

She made her way to the kitchen and stepped into the moccasins she'd abandoned there the night before, then pushed open the back door. Mariah wished it didn't creak so loudly. She'd have to give it another lubrication.

It was an oft-repeated repair, made necessary by the blowing desert grit and red dust that made its way into every crack and crevice around here. But Mariah didn't mind. She loved the old place.

She started toward the driveway where Luke had unloaded the cycle from the bed of her truck, and had a half dozen parts spread over the sparse grass.

He didn't hear her approach, and for a moment she let her gaze linger on his tall, muscled frame. He worked in his newly fashioned cutoffs of last night, a denim shirt and well-broken-in sneakers, the white of the shoes and the laces already coated with the perennial, high-desert red dust.

For a brief moment she could see him belonging here in this untamed country—with the rugged red rocks, its scruffy trees and the surrounding mountains. She could see him belonging here—with Callie and her.

But she quickly eradicated that thought from her mind.

Luke didn't belong here; he was only passing through.

Maybe it was the way he looked in his denim shirt, his deep tan and windblown hair that had fooled her senses. She ordered herself to think rationally.

"Hi," she called out as she neared. "What has you up so early? Didn't you sleep well?"

He turned to face her, looking a little surprised to see her, then his gaze trailed over her slowly, lazily, and his mouth crooked into a pleased half smile.

Mariah felt every inch of his smile.

And his gaze.

"I slept all right, until one *insufferable* raven decided to become my personal alarm clock."

Mariah felt a laugh bubble up. The bird was a nuisance, but he seemed to have found a home here. Probably because Callie fed him—which destroyed any chance of him flying off to torment some other family, Mariah was sure.

"You mean Bandit? I should have warned you about him."

"Bandit?"

She smiled. "Callie named him that. Making noise isn't his only bad habit. If you leave one of those tiny silver parts lying about, it'll soon be missing."

"The bird is a thief?"

"With no conscience, I'm afraid." She glanced down at the metal part in his hand. "What are you doing? Assessing the damage from yesterday?"

She wasn't sure how he'd unloaded the cycle from the back of her truck without help, but Luke was strong and muscular. Still, he shouldn't have risked tearing open the laceration on his leg or putting strain on his shoulder.

"I'm trying to fix it. I need to leave, Mariah."

His tone carried such resolve that it jolted her senses. She knew he'd be leaving, but still his words struck her with the force of a truck slamming into a mountain.

If she hadn't allowed that kiss last night, hadn't responded to him the way she had, maybe she wouldn't be so thrown off balance now. "How soon?" she asked.

His gaze slid over her, and she read something indefinable in his eyes.

Was he, too, regretting their kiss?

Was there something—or someone—drawing him to the road?

"Tonight," he answered. "If I can figure out how to get the bike in running order by then."

"Tonight?" Mariah's voice sounded like Bandit's, at the bird's most annoying, she was sure. But she couldn't believe he'd even *think* of getting back on his bike before he'd had a chance to recover. "You're not in any shape to ride again that soon. Your leg, your shoulder— you need time to heal."

He turned back to his bike, seemingly ignoring her concern. "So I'll be a little uncomfortable," he said. "I'm sure I'll survive."

Mariah wanted to spin him around to face her, make him listen to reason, but he was absorbed in fitting some part to the silver machine. "Luke Phillips, I am *not* in the habit of patching up people only to have my handiwork undone. The least you can do is give your cuts and bruises another day or two."

The woman looked like a small firecracker exploding with fury. She was concerned about him. She cared. And that hit him where he lived. It had been a long time since anyone had cared what happened to him.

But Mariah did.

He knew she was right about his injuries. His thigh still hurt like the very devil, and his shoulder had stiffened up on him. Still, he couldn't stick around. He had to keep moving—always hoping relief, peace, was just over the next rise.

Mariah had treated his wounds with her herbs and salves, but Luke had battle scars worse than those, scars none of her medicines could heal.

"I've infringed on your hospitality enough. I need to move on," he said.

He couldn't explain anything beyond that. He couldn't even explain it to himself. His heart ached from his son's death, an anguish so deep he didn't think he'd ever get over the pain. Mariah was a healer with her special medicines, but she couldn't heal his deeper pain, couldn't exorcise his guilt.

He turned back to the cycle—and the part he wasn't at all sure he could render usable again. He didn't know much about mechanics; he only knew bodies—or at least he once had.

The little bit he knew about motorcycles he'd picked up from repair manuals, like the one he'd packed up and put in storage, along with everything else he owned.

How could he have known that he'd be felled by an armadillo the size of a...humvee?

"Luke, you haven't infringed on my hospitality." Her voice was low and soft—and did damage to Luke's senses.

She didn't leave, but stood watching him work. He felt her presence, caught her sweet scent on the light breeze. Hospitality infringed or not—he couldn't stick around. Mariah was too tempting.

Last night's kiss had proven that.

"Can I bring you some coffee? Or can you quit for a while and come in for breakfast?"

He heard her sweet offer and straightened up, wrench in hand. He was getting nowhere fast with his repair job. "I'm not hungry, but a cup of coffee would be nice," he told her.

She nodded, and then left.

He watched her go, realizing he was accepting her kindness once again. When the back door closed behind her he felt a sense of loss, like the sun slipping behind a cloud, dampening the spirit. With an inaudible groan, he dragged his gaze back to the cycle—and the work ahead of him.

A short while later Mariah was back, a white mug in hand. He stopped his work and took it from her, trying not to touch her hand in the process. The merest brush would set off fire in his veins, fire that would lick at his already flailing resolve.

"Thanks," he said, managing the exchange without incident. But the smile in her green eyes stoked his libido, and he nearly dropped the mug.

"If you want a refill, the pot's on the kitchen counter. Callie's awake, so I need to tend to her," she said, and quickly disappeared back indoors.

Again Luke felt the loss of sunshine.

He took a sip of the coffee she'd brought him. It was a good rich brew, dark and strong—like the stuff that had kept him going many a long night at the hospital.

But Luke didn't want to think about that, about medicine, the hospital.

Or the reason he'd left it all behind.

A few hours later Luke was still working on his bike. Apparently the man was determined to ignore her reminder that his injuries needed a little time to heal before he rode off to...to wherever it was he planned to go.

Callie was resting, playing with her dolls on the bed. Rest periods were one thing Mariah insisted on as part of her daughter's health regimen. Often she got overly tired from too much playing and running around. She needed the frequent quiet times to keep her body in harmony.

Mariah reached for her gardening gloves and headed for her garden at the side of the house. She was glad the morning was still pleasant. A late June breeze blew, and the sun wasn't yet high in the sky. In the afternoon it would be too hot to work.

She'd promised Callie a picnic by the stream for their lunch. Maybe she'd invite Luke to join them. He'd been busy with his cycle all morning—and his leg and shoulder could use a respite. Especially if he foolishly planned to leave tonight.

He didn't seem to be aware of her working nearby, so intent was he on his repairs. He'd stripped off his blue denim shirt, she noticed, and sweat sheened his body. Sunlight danced off his tanned skin. Again she wondered at his life, the pain she read in his eyes.

What had caused it?

And was it a pain too great for time to heal?

Considering the way Luke affected her, maybe she was better off not knowing. She could still taste his kiss from last night. And watching him work in the sun, his body hard and glistening, made her foolish heart lurch.

She tore her gaze away, back to the harsh soil she was aerating. Luke Phillips was a man determined to be on his way—off to wherever the road would take him.

And Mariah's life would return to normal.

Luke glanced up from his bike. Was he making any headway with the thing? He wasn't sure he was. He grabbed a blue bandana from his back pocket and mopped the sweat from his face.

It was getting damned hot out here, he thought, as he tied the bandanna around his forehead, hoping to keep the sweat from dripping into his eyes.

He'd caught a quick glimpse of Mariah as she'd headed toward her garden at the side of the house, but he'd tried not to let the distraction take hold.

He needed to keep busy, his thoughts on what he was doing. He needed transportation, the luxury of riding out of here—hoping he could find a measure of solace in the very act of meeting the wind head-on and riding to no place.

And if not that, at least he wouldn't be around Mariah, tempting her with hot, hungry kisses that held no promise of anything but the present.

He risked a quick glance in her direction. She was tilling the soil around a small plant as if it were precious gold—and to Mariah it probably was. She fit here, he realized. In this world, among her living things, on the earth that she tended with such care.

He suspected everything she touched thrived under her attention. Her touch was healing, but to Luke it was more. From the merest brush of her hand to that soft kiss that had devastated him last night, it was raw temptation.

What would it be like to make love with her? To have her feast her eyes on him, wanting him, just him? What would it be like to sample her sweetness, feel her come alive in his arms, to slide into her warm, lithe body?

He dragged his mind away from the dangerous thought.

She appeared the picture of coolness as she worked, as if the heat of the sun didn't affect her in the slightest. As if she were somehow immune.

Luke wished he had a little of that immunity, immunity to who and what she was—a healer, a sorceress, an enchantress, who could make a man want what he shouldn't want.

Just then she glanced up and caught his gaze on her, her green eyes mesmerizing and beautiful as they studied him, those eyes that attested to a mixed heritage in her background.

What had it been like for her growing up on the Rez?

She made him curious.

He knew she was curious about him, as well, who he was, why he was on his long trip to nowhere, but she was too polite to ask him questions.

And if she did ask, what answers could he give?

How could anyone understand what he was going through, the hated sense of failing someone you loved more than life itself? Of being a man of medicine and not being able to stop the life from seeping out of your own child's body?

He tried to shove the memory aside—not to forget what had happened, not to forget his son, but to store it away until he was stronger.

Until he could forgive himself.

The late-morning sun glinted down on her, making her hair gleam like luxurious silk. If he could delve his fingers into it, seek another kiss like last night, would he be able to forget?

Just a little?

"Are you ready for lunch?" she called out to him. Her voice was melodic—and inviting. "I promised Callie a picnic by the stream. And you need to give your leg and shoulder a rest."

He wasn't having a whole lot of luck with his bike— and he'd been at it since sunup. Maybe he could use a break. A picnic. Luke couldn't recall ever having had a picnic before.

Suddenly that seemed like a major omission in his life.

"Can I help with anything?" he asked.

A smile widened her mouth. "Not a thing. Just come in and wash up."

He glanced down at his grease-covered fingers. The

rest of him wasn't a whole lot cleaner. And he probably smelled like a wild goat to boot.

"That'll take some doing," he said, but he tossed his wrench aside and followed her to the back door.

"The shower is that way. I'll go see about Callie," she said and disappeared in the direction of her daughter's bedroom.

Luke found the shower just off the kitchen and turned on the hot water. He hated to admit it, but Mariah was right about his injuries. They were far from healed. His shoulder throbbed and his leg wound had begun to bleed again.

But he'd be damned if he'd let her sweet hands touch him a second time. He'd find the gauze and tape and dress his own wounds. It was safer.

Much safer.

Callie had fallen asleep on her bed, amidst her pile of dolls and dollclothes. Mariah hated to wake her. She must have gotten overly tired yesterday with Luke here. Any new excitement often meant fatigue for her daughter.

Quietly Mariah backed out of the room and closed Callie's door. She'd let her sleep while she fixed their lunch and packed the picnic hamper, then she'd wake her.

She heard the shower running as she made up chicken-salad sandwiches on thick bread with lettuce and slices of tomato. She made a peanut butter and jelly sandwich for Callie—her favorite—and cut it into quarters just the way she liked it.

She rinsed red grapes and put them in a colander to drain while she packed silverware, napkins and milk for Callie. Then, on a thought, she added a bottle of white wine for Luke and her, along with a pair of mismatched glass goblets.

She put in some of Una's homemade tortillas, then, rooting around in the fridge, she found yellow cheese, which she cut into wedges and wrapped in foil. She stood back and wondered if anything was missing.

A tablecloth, she remembered, and dug in a bottom kitchen drawer to retrieve the blue-checked one reserved for her and Callie's many lunches.

"Looks like you're packing enough food for an army."

The deep velvet voice came from behind her.

Mariah spun around to face Luke, hair damp from his shower, dressed in only his denim cutoffs, a blue towel hanging around his neck. The scrape on his face looked better, she thought, trying to focus on anything but gorgeous male.

Instead what came to her senses was the memory of patching him up last night, his closeness and body heat. She brushed her fingers along his jaw as if her very touch could heal the wound.

Her hand trailed to his shoulder. The heat of the water from his shower had heightened the bruising. He sported a dozen wild colors, ranging from yellow to green to black. "Is it painful?" she asked.

What had happened to her therapeutic skills, seeing what needed to be done, and doing it, without her mind and her senses getting in the way?

Of course, she'd never had a patient like Luke Phillips before, a man so tempting, so virile, he set off alarm bells in her head.

"Would I admit it if it was?"

He was teasing her, being the macho male. His blue

eyes were dark with something she couldn't quite define, or maybe she was afraid to. His smile was slow and dangerous, and Mariah suddenly felt a little wobbly—as if an earthquake threatened her balance.

He drew a deep breath and stepped away. "I'll go to the cabin and put on fresh clothes," he said.

He turned to leave.

"Wait—your leg. You'll need a dressing."

"All taken care of, Doc." He raised the ragged edge of his cutoffs and showed her the new gauze bandage he sported. "I found your medical supplies in the cabinet."

Mariah let out a cowardly sigh of relief. She wouldn't have to endanger her hormones doing the task herself. Luke stole her breath away, set her heart to pounding, and her knees to shaking.

She swallowed hard.

In a few minutes he'd be back, hungry for lunch.

And she still had to wake Callie.

She stopped in the small bathroom and checked her appearance in the mirror. Her green eyes were wide, a hint sultry. From Luke's effect on her?

Yes.

She needed to keep her wits about her and not lose her head over a man she barely knew, a man on his way to somewhere else.

"I'm so hungry I could eat barbecued raven," Luke said, standing by the back door as Mariah and Callie emerged.

Callie laughed. "I hope you don't mean Bandit," she said, hopping down the steps ahead of her mother. "I like him."

"Hmm—*Bandit?* Is he that *huuu-mmmon-gous*, black, silky-feathered, caterwauling bird who hangs out here and woke me up this morning?" he asked, knowing Callie would recognize her raven from his silly description. "A bird about *thiiiiis* long, and meaner than the very devil." He expanded his hands to indicate size.

Callie giggled. "That's Bandit, but he's not *mean*. And he doesn't cater-cater-wol," she informed him.

"Says who?"

"Says *me*. I feed him—and he likes that."

"Okay—I won't eat him, then. As long as your mom has something good to eat in that basket."

"She does," Callie announced. "My mommy makes good picnics."

Luke didn't doubt that. Everything Mariah did was done with care and love. And he wondered how the hell he was going to get through this picnic without being tempted to kiss her again.

He couldn't remember any other woman who intrigued him the way Mariah did. Even doing simple, everyday things seemed special when he did them with her—sitting at the small kitchen table to eat a bowl of homemade chili, helping with the dishes afterward, taking a walk through the cool night air.

Sharing a kiss.

Sharing a kiss—that was where Luke had gotten in trouble. That kiss had sent him to the repairs his bike desperately needed first thing this morning.

And it still wasn't fixed.

They walked side by side in companionable silence toward the picnic spot, Callie bouncing along ahead of them on her awkward braces. The little girl impressed him. She didn't let much hamper her, didn't let anything dampen her spirit.

And Luke wished he could find some of that resilience for himself.

Along with a little of Callie's sunshine.

His heart still ached at the sight of small children. But somehow with Callie it was different. She didn't make his heart ache. If anything she gave him strength—just seeing it in her.

He missed Dane with a father's ache in his heart. The son who would never grow up and take his place in the world. And Luke needed to find a way to live with that.

And with his guilt.

They reached the spot by the stream, and Mariah spread an old quilt on the ground, then placed the blue-and-white checkered cloth over the top of it.

Luke and Callie investigated the stream while she unpacked their lunch. She heard Callie's giggle and Luke's deep laugh and wondered what had prompted their merriment.

Callie had really taken to him—and Mariah wasn't sure that was a good thing. She didn't want her daughter getting overly attached to a man who'd be leaving soon.

It had taken Callie a long time to get over her father's leaving. Though now she rarely mentioned him. And Mariah was glad. Thinking of Will, and how he'd turned his back on both of them, still hurt her—deeply.

Though more for Callie's sake than for her own.

It would be nice to have a man in her life someday, a man who'd love her—and Callie.

A man with staying power.

But there were few men around Sunrise.

She told herself having Callie was enough for her, that they were a family, a small family, but still a family. She loved her daughter. And Callie loved her.

But sometimes Mariah longed for something more.

Sometimes she longed for a kiss like the one she'd shared with Luke last night. Sometimes she longed for a man to curl up next to, a man to wake her in the morning, wanting her body and her heart. A man she could believe in and who believed in her.

A man who loved her.

Luke had resurrected dangerous feelings in her, dangerous wants, reminding her there was more to experience in life. More joy. More excitement.

There was desire. Loving. A sexual side to her femininity.

Forget that, Mariah, she told herself.

She had peace, happiness, the joy of being a mother. And that was enough—at least for now. She wasn't ready to risk what she already had for what she *thought* she wanted.

Finally Luke and Callie returned, drawn, no doubt, by the promise of food. The pair was still chatting as they sat down on the blanket. Callie's small face was alight with excitement—and Luke's dark look had faded. And Mariah was glad. Nature could be a salve for any soul.

Even Luke's?

She hoped so.

Her herbs could mend bodily injuries, but it took more than herbs to heal the pain of the soul. If Mariah knew how to alleviate Luke's pain, even a little, she would try.

Though, with the way he could affect her senses, she

knew she should back away. The man could make her vulnerable in a way even Will had not.

She couldn't risk her heart again.

"Mmm—this looks delicious," Luke said, glancing from the array of food in front of him to Mariah. "Thanks for including me in this picnic."

There was heat in his smile and something else, something that raced along Mariah's veins, warning her that he was a danger to her carefully guarded heart.

Just seeing that smile on his lips reminded her of the taste of his kiss last night. The taste and the forbidden excitement.

"I hope you enjoy it," she said, bringing herself back down to earth.

She couldn't allow herself to get swept up in the man and his appeal. He'd be here only until he'd repaired his bike.

Then he'd leave—and become nothing more than a memory in her and Callie's life.

Chapter Five

Luke didn't know when he'd enjoyed himself more. He was glad Mariah had invited him. He tried a bite of the cheese she'd packed, and leaned back on one elbow to sip his wine and bask in the quiet of the afternoon.

Callie had finished her lunch and was restless to play. "Mommy, can I go wade in the stream?" she asked.

Mariah offered the little girl a smile, and Luke had never seen such mother-love on a woman's face before—and he'd come across many worried moms in the trauma unit.

Right now the hospital, his life in Chicago, seemed a million miles away from this little corner of the world. He'd been the top doctor in the E.R., had it all—or so he'd thought. Now he knew he'd had damned little.

He'd enjoyed the accolades the med center bestowed on him, his title as chief of trauma, the power meetings and everything wealth afforded him, but in the end it meant nothing.

Not without Dane.

Mariah nodded at her daughter. "Okay, Callie—but don't get your clothes wet. I don't want you to get sick."

"I won't, Mommy—I promise."

"And be careful," she added as she watched Callie bound off toward the stream.

The admonition was gentle, though. Mariah didn't know any way *but* gentle, Luke suspected. She was wonderful with Callie, and with the disability that faced her child. He knew she worried, but as far as Luke could see, it was an unnecessary concern for the most part.

Callie did need Mariah's extra attention because of her illness, but she was an inspiring little girl, a little girl who could easily capture Luke's heart.

Her mother could, as well.

Callie sat down at the water's edge and undid her braces with an expertise born of necessity, then stepped gingerly out onto the stream's flat stones.

Luke turned to Mariah, who had been following her daughter's actions as he had been. "You're a good mother, Mariah. You do very well with Callie."

She turned to glance at him. Her cheeks held a warm blush. "Thanks—it isn't always easy."

He wondered in what way she meant that. Nothing in Mariah's life looked easy to Luke, yet she managed it all with an innate grace and beauty.

"Tell me about Callie's father," he said quietly.

He admitted he was curious, though he knew he shouldn't be. He wouldn't be around long enough to earn the right to ask questions.

Or to get the answers to them.

"We're divorced," she said, as if the failure had been hers somehow. She reached for her wineglass, swirling the light-colored contents inside. "Will couldn't deal with Callie's illness, the doctor bills, the extra attention she needed. So one day he…he just packed up and left."

There wasn't any bitterness in her voice, only a resoluteness that she'd be there for her daughter. Luke admired her strength, her determination. Mariah was special; he'd known that from the first moment he saw her out there on that mesa.

But her words reminded him of his own failing, his inability to save his child—or to live with the consequences. Where could he find some of that strength that seemed to come so naturally to her?

Did she find it in her herbs, her healing, the earth?

Was there some magic potion that could help him take on the hardships of life the way she did? Or was it deep within the soul and the trick was to reach within and find it?

Whichever it was, Mariah had found it. She'd take on the world for her daughter without a worry for herself.

"Do you ever hear from him?" he asked.

She shook her head. "Not anymore. In the beginning he sent some money. He apparently had a job in California where he'd gone. Now, I don't hear anything from him."

Nor did she want to, Luke imagined. She'd written the man off and taken up the reins herself. He could see it in the proud jut of her chin, the determination in her soft green eyes.

"What about you, Luke Phillips—have you ever been married?"

A million years ago. He and Sylvie had been all wrong for each other. The only good that had come of their marriage was Dane—but now Dane was gone.

"Once," he said. "We were divorced several years ago."

"Do you have any children?"

Her upturned face sought the answer, the answer he didn't know how to give. How could he explain something he didn't yet know how to deal with?

"No," he said, the word a rasp in his throat, the pain having dried up his voice. "No children."

"A girlfriend?"

Luke gave a small laugh. He could field that one more easily. "No girlfriend."

"I'm sorry," she said. "I guess this sounds like an interrogation."

"There's no need to be sorry. I started it with my nosy question."

"I suppose you did. More wine?" she asked.

"Mmm, yes." Luke reached for the bottle, removed the cork and refilled both their glasses. "Here's to the picnic—and the woman who made it wonderful."

He tilted his glass to hers, though she responded uncertainly to his toast. "I'm afraid it wasn't much, but Callie loves a picnic, so we do it often."

"You made me give my injuries a rest," he said, "but now I'm way behind on my bike repair."

"Luke…" She looked somewhat hesitant, then her chin rose. "You're welcome to the cabin—and our hospitality as long as you need it. Unless there's somewhere you have to be, something you need to do, don't rush the healing. Don't leave too soon. Not on my account."

Oh, God! Luke thought. It was precisely on her account he *should* leave. Mariah was too tempting for any man, too sweet, too special. Her earthy beauty filled his head with fantasies he didn't dare allow to play out.

"There's no place I have to be. Still, I need to leave, Mariah. There are things I have…to work out. And maybe, just maybe, I can find some answers on my way."

Like Will, Mariah thought as a mental punch hit her in the stomach. Will had said nearly the same thing to her—and broke her heart.

Along with Callie's.

But, despite his words, Luke was nothing like Will. She knew that.

Will had left because he was a weak man. Luke wasn't weak in any way. But he did have demons he was fighting. She could read that in his troubled blue eyes, see it in his face.

Something—or someone—had hurt him to his very soul.

She was glad he'd shared that small admission with her. It was the first sign of healing.

"If you have to go, then let me take care of those cuts and scrapes before you do. I-I'd like to know you'll be all right."

Mariah heard his quick intake of air, as if he thought that a risky idea. And remembering last night, and the effects of her hands on him, perhaps he was right.

She was always calm, cool and professional with those she treated—but she'd never treated someone like Luke before. Someone who could swamp her senses the way he did. But she wouldn't let it happen a second time.

She would be in control.

"Thanks, but I'll be fine, Mariah."

He stroked his thumb across her cheek, sending tiny explosions of need through her so quick and powerful it stole her breath. Then he drew her close, so close Mariah could feel his heat, the scent of male, *powerful* male.

How could any woman be around Luke and not respond to him?

Especially a woman who ran across few of his species here in the Arizona desert?

He touched her lips briefly with his—and she was certain she'd never felt anything so sensual in her life. It was a mere brush, but the tug on her senses was powerful. Her lips trembled beneath his and her hormones flared.

He drew back and Mariah followed, wanting his lips pressed to hers one more time. She felt as parched for passion as the dry desert was for rainfall.

And Luke was delicious rain.

His lips brushed hers again, this time followed with a low, agonizing moan—his moan. Though it could well have been her own; she wanted him that much.

"Oh God, Mariah, you make me *want*."

His words, his breath, stroked her lips. Heat raced to her core, igniting deep fire. She very much wanted another kiss, even more from this man, but Callie was playing nearby.

They weren't alone.

And she had no business wanting anything from Luke Phillips.

"I know," she said in a soft whisper. "I shouldn't have pressed."

"I started it. Don't blame yourself."

But she did. She wasn't free for a fling, an affair, not even a simple kiss. Luke was leaving, perhaps as early as tonight. That was something she needed to remember—before she ended up with her heart trampled in the Arizona dust.

She drew away from him, then stood up. "I—I need to get Callie."

Luke watched her walk toward the water's edge and her daughter. His body throbbed with hardened need, need for this beautiful woman and the peace she so easily brought.

Her soft-washed jeans hugged her fanny enticingly, and her hair hung to her waist, a silky free fall the color of rich mahogany. He could have gone on kissing her for a week.

He'd never known a woman who could tempt him the way Mariah did. Was it her innocence, her gentleness, her compassion? Or was it her beauty, her femininity, the taste of her sweet lips?

All he knew was he couldn't take his gaze from her.

He smiled at Callie's protest as the water rippled over her fragile ankles. Obviously the child wanted to play longer, but at her mother's insistence, she clambered onto the bank.

Mariah gave her a hug, then bent to dry the little girl's feet with her towel and replace her unwieldy braces. Callie could walk without them, but Luke knew they protected the little girl's tender joints by cushioning her movements.

Luke had seen bravery in many forms before, but never had the sight of it moved him so much.

They were a pair, mother and daughter, in tune with each other, sharing their strength and their spirit—with no real need for a man to lean on.

"Did you see me splashing in the water?" Callie asked him as she tumbled onto the blanket a few moments later.

He tweaked her cute little nose. "Was that you, princess? I thought it was a hop-toad."

Callie giggled, and laughter shimmered in her green eyes, so like her mother's. "I'm not a hop-toad," she said with insistence.

"You're *not*—well, you could've fooled me."

Callie's eyes were bright, her smile a delight. She had warmed to Luke easily, a child who trusted—though she'd had a lot of pain in her short life.

He glanced from the little girl to her mother. Mariah's gaze was soft, and a smile curved at her pretty lips. It was easy to see that Callie was her world.

He thought of Dane—and how their father-son world had been shattered so quickly, so permanently. The pain caught his breath, stealing life from him as surely as the accident had stolen his son from him.

He swallowed hard and forced a smile. He didn't want to ruin a little girl's happy afternoon. Or *his* happy afternoon. He'd enjoyed the day, as well.

Mariah saw a stab of pain in Luke's eyes. It sneaked up on him when he didn't expect it, as it had just now. Perhaps, if she didn't take such notice of the man, she wouldn't be so aware of what she saw there in his eyes, that shadow of sadness, a sadness of the soul that shouldn't be there.

What had hurt him that badly?

Made him feel he'd never be whole again?

But she knew that wasn't something he was ready to share.

She stood up. "Okay, sweetheart," she said to her daughter, "lunch is over and you need your rest time."

"I know," she answered dejectedly.

Luke stood, too, and helped Callie to her feet, carefully steadying her on her braces. He seemed so attuned to Callie's disability, so unlike Will. And Mariah wondered what made Luke different.

Who was he?

The man filled her with questions, more questions than he'd probably ever answer.

"You heard your mom, princess," he said. "And she's the boss."

"I know," Callie said again.

Mariah hated always having to be the ogre to her daughter, hated that Callie couldn't be a carefree child like other kids her age—but Mariah knew the consequences of too much activity.

And that, she hated, too.

She reached for the blanket to fold it. Luke caught one end of it to help her, and their fingers brushed in the process. Mariah felt the jolt at his touch. Why did she react to him the way she did?

Why had she kissed him again?

And why had she enjoyed it so much?

She draped the now-folded blanket over her arm and allowed Luke to carry the hamper. Callie skipped ahead of them, apparently already having forgotten that Mariah had called a halt to her fun—for which Mariah was glad.

Luke matched her stride as they climbed the hill to the house. Mariah was all too aware of him beside her, his body agile, his scent purely masculine.

Her awareness of him as a man tingled through her and she drew in a deep breath, hoping to steady her nerves—and her senses. Luke was far too sexy for a woman to ignore.

He was also kind and gentle with Callie, anticipating her needs, understanding her deficiencies. There weren't very many men like him in this world.

But Luke was on his way to somewhere else, she reminded herself.

And in a hurry to do it, as well.

The afternoon sun was beginning to bake Luke's back and neck, the shade from the scrawny cottonwood tree woefully inadequate as he worked on his Harley. Damn, but it was hot in these parts. Even Mariah had retreated from her gardening chores and escaped to the cool interior of the house.

He wiped the sweat from his forehead with the back of his arm and gave the surroundings a slow glance as if expecting to see the devil himself guarding fires with a pitchfork.

Okay, so maybe it wasn't *that* hot.

But it was close.

Then Luke saw a young kid of eleven, maybe twelve, bounding across the backyard in his direction. The boy was all gangly arms and legs. His brown eyes were full of curiosity—about Luke and the motorcycle.

Especially the cycle.

He'd come from next door—Una's house. Her

grandson, Eli, Luke suspected. Mariah had mentioned him.

"Hi," Luke greeted him. "Do you know anything about fixing bikes?"

He expected the boy to shake his head.

Instead he nodded. "My dad says I can fix anything."

Luke's luck was changing—*if* the kid was right about his brilliance. Of course, it didn't take a lot of brilliance to be better with a bike than Luke. All he knew was how to ride. He left the mechanics to someone else. "I'm Luke," he said, extending his hand.

The boy shook it. "I know. My grandmother told me. I'm Eli."

"Well, Eli, do you think you can help me get this machine up and running again?"

The boy's eyes were bright. "You mean it?"

Luke meant it.

He handed Eli a wrench and showed him the front wheel section that had been damaged when he'd swerved to miss that armadillo.

The boy gave the wheel a studious glance, then began systematically dismantling parts.

Luke hoped like hell the kid knew what he was doing or he'd never get on down the highway—and away from the temptation Mariah represented. His willpower where this woman was concerned was worthless, and he didn't need to add another complication to his life.

He was dealing with enough already.

"What do you think, champ?" he asked, turning his attention back to Eli and the cycle he was working hard at.

Eli held up a dismantled part. "I think this is your problem."

Luke stared at the piece Eli was holding aloft—the front wheel brake. The *much-needed* front wheel brake. The kid claimed he could pound out the dents inflicted on the other parts, but the brake was critical.

And Luke knew he was right.

He didn't know whether to be happy the problem was solved or disgruntled because the kid was a better tool man. "How old are you?" he asked.

"I'll be thirteen next month."

Yep, Luke's pride was definitely wounded.

"There's only one problem," the boy said.

Only one? Why did Luke think that wasn't good news? "Okay—what's the problem?" he asked.

"I don't know where you'll find one around here."

Luke couldn't say that surprised him. Maybe Mariah would lend him her truck.

And what...? he wondered. Would he have to drive all the way to Phoenix to locate what he needed?

He sighed heavily.

"Sorry," the boy said.

"Yeah, me, too, kid."

Eli ran a hand over the silver chrome. "It's a cool bike, though. How fast will she do?"

Luke had ridden it flat out at ninety, determined to outrun his pain, the memories of his son, the reminder that he hadn't been able to save him. But he couldn't tell Eli that.

"Not fast enough to dodge an armadillo in the road," he grumbled.

The boy laughed. "My grandmother told me what happened."

Great, Luke thought. The whole damn town probably

knew what had brought him down. He wouldn't be able to hold his head up around here.

It was a good thing he was leaving soon.

Or was he?

"I'd like to have a bike like this someday," Eli said, a tenor of longing in his voice.

"Well, maybe you will—when you get a little older."

The kid didn't look very hopeful. Luke suspected money was short in the boy's family—and he felt for him.

"Maybe I'll open a cycle repair shop. Then I can have a bike as well as fix them."

"Smart thinking," Luke said. The boy had the talent for it. He knew what to do with a wrench in his hand. But Luke knew dreams didn't always turn out as expected. He'd achieved his easily enough, only to have them shatter into a million pieces.

What would Dane's future have been? Med school? Law school? Engineering? *Don't go down that road,* Luke admonished himself.

He centered his thoughts on Eli instead. "How about school?" he asked. "Are you any good at math? You'll need to keep records for that bike shop and you'll have to be good at it."

Luke wondered how he'd gotten himself into this— but he knew how. He liked Eli—and wanted to help.

"I get okay grades in math, but…"

"But what?"

"I don't like school very much."

Luke hadn't, either, at that age—but he didn't think he should tell the kid that. Instead he gave him a stern glance. "It'll be pretty hard to get that shop you want then."

He didn't mean to be hard on the boy, but Eli didn't

seem to have family around to give him encouragement, except for Una. And Mariah. Mariah treated
him like family, but then that was her way. She'd even
taken Luke in.

"Maybe school's not so bad," the boy said finally and
Luke hid a smile at the kid's acquiescence.

Just then they both glanced up to see Mariah walking
toward them. Luke's heart bucked at the sight of her. She
looked as cool as a cucumber, despite the afternoon's
hot temperature. She'd pulled her hair up off her pretty
neck in deference to the heat and fastened it with a clip.
Luke knew the luxurious feel of it, its thickness, even
its scent. And he'd love to loosen the clasp that held it
up and let it tumble into his hands.

"How are the repairs going?" she asked.

Her gaze traveled from Luke to Eli, then back to
Luke again, her green eyes soft and questioning as they
brushed him.

"Not well," Luke complained.

"No...? Eli's pretty good with repairs," she returned
and smiled at the boy.

He brightened like a high-wattage bulb, both at her
praise and her attention. In fact, he nearly fell all over
himself. Luke couldn't blame him for the reaction.

Luke's was just as sappy.

"Oh, he's very good. He found the problem with the
bike right off. Unfortunately it wasn't the outcome I'd
hoped for." He held up the damaged brake line as proof
of his words. "Know where I might get one of these?"

"Right offhand? No."

Luke grimaced. "That's what I was afraid of."

"But I do know where two guys can get a glass of

lemonade while they contemplate the situation," she said, offering them each a small smile.

Luke knew there was little they could do until he'd located the needed part. And he could use a cold drink and the cool of Mariah's kitchen.

"C'mon, champ," he said to Eli. "Before the lady changes her mind."

Mariah added ice to three tall glasses, then picked up the pitcher and poured the lemonade into each and topped them with a sprig of fresh mint from her herb garden.

"Thanks," Eli said when she handed him his glass. "I really like your lemonade."

Mariah smiled. It didn't taste any different than his grandmother's, but she accepted the compliment anyway. Eli was a good kid. She liked him—and all the help he gave her in the garden.

She knew the boy had a crush on her, but give him a year or two, and some cute young girl would steal him away.

And Mariah would lose a good gardener.

She gave him and Luke a quick smile, then took her seat and sipped her own drink. "So, what are your plans for a new part?" she asked the two of them.

Eli shrugged his young shoulders and glanced at Luke.

Luke squirmed a bit in his chair. "I was hoping you might loan me your truck. I may have to drive to Phoenix to find a repair shop."

"You're welcome to the truck, but you might try Cottonwood for it first. It's a much shorter drive."

"Good," he said. "You and Callie want to ride along? We could make a day of it."

Mariah thought about it. Cottonwood wasn't so far for Callie to travel—and her daughter would love the outing. She'd also love riding along with Luke.

And Mariah…?

How did she feel about spending the day with Luke?

She needed to keep a tight rein on her senses around him—but she'd also enjoy the trip. "If we go early. In the morning, before the heat of the day sets in," she said.

He smiled as if it were some sort of special date between them, then turned to Eli. "Thanks for all your help this afternoon, champ—and if you're around tomorrow, I could sure use your expertise putting the new part into operation."

Eli's face lit up at the prospect of the job. "That'd be awesome."

Mariah couldn't help but smile at Eli's enthusiasm. And Una would be glad her grandson had something that interested him. He didn't have a male influence in his life, at least not a *good* one. His father drank too much, which worried Una—and it also worried Mariah.

Drinking was a big problem for her people, both on and off the Rez. It was the lack of jobs—and the lack of hope that something good could happen in their life that made men like Eli's father drink. The Hopi were a proud people—and when they couldn't provide for their family, it exacted a toll.

"Thanks for the lemonade," Eli said, pushing aside his empty glass. "My grandmother's expecting me home for dinner." He scooted back his chair and got to his feet. "And thanks for letting me work on your bike," he added to Luke.

Luke gave him a wink. "No, champ," he said. "Thank *you* for helping."

A big grin filled Eli's face, and Mariah was sure the boy stood two inches taller.

"See you tomorrow, Luke," he said and slipped out the back door toward home.

"That was one wonderful thing you did," she told Luke.

"Hey, the kid's the wonderful one," he said, deflecting her praise. "He's a complete whiz at this stuff. Without him I'd still be out there sweating in the sun."

"I think you're being modest," she said, not buying his sidestep of the issue.

"I'm no saint, Mariah. Don't paint me as one."

Mariah tried to read his face, wondering why he thought so little of himself. She took a sip of her lemonade then set it down. "All the same, thanks for your kindness to him. He's been…troubled lately."

"Oh—why?"

Mariah wasn't sure how much to say, but Luke had been good to the boy. "Eli lost his mother a few years ago. His father, Jimmy, is a good man but since his wife's death his drinking has…escalated. Una tries hard to be the strength in the boy's life, but she worries about the situation."

"Losing his mother, then seeing his father drink too much? That's tough for any kid to deal with."

"I know."

Luke could see the concern in Mariah's eyes. She had her own problems, yet she had room in her heart to worry about others. She was a special woman. Certainly like no other woman he'd known. Which was why he needed to repair his bike and ride out of here.

Before he fell for her.

Luke—a man with an empty soul.

Chapter Six

Luke was certain he smelled plenty rank after working in the hot sun all afternoon. He stepped into the shower—but Mariah followed him into it.

Well, maybe not literally—but definitely in his rampant thoughts.

He could feel her softness, the pulsing water from the shower and the fragrant soap she'd milled with her special herbs making their bodies slick and aware. It was getting harder to restrain his wanton desire for the desert beauty.

She was a fantasy that was real, a fantasy he had touched, taken into his arms and kissed. But Luke needed to forget those kisses, forget the way she'd responded to him.

Mariah was fragile, an innocent who'd already been hurt by one man. She needed someone better than Luke.

She needed a man who would stick around and slay dragons for her.

She'd gone to wake Callie from her nap and give her the fresh herbal drink she'd fixed for her. Mariah swore by it and Callie seemed to thrive on its medicinal properties. But then, everything Mariah did was healing.

Was it her medicine or her touch that worked such magic?

Luke was sorely tempted to stick around and find out, but no matter what her talents were, they couldn't heal the anguish Luke carried in his heart.

She'd offered him friendship, rescued him when he'd sorely needed it. He couldn't abuse her trust, that innocence, no matter how badly he wanted her.

Until his bike was fixed and he could ride out of here, that was the way he intended to keep things between them—simple and uncomplicated.

He rinsed off the soap, letting the spray pepper his body with sharp, hot needles. It would be tough enough leaving here with no more regrets than he'd ridden in with.

But he was determined to do so.

Somehow.

Mariah had finished giving Callie her "healthy drink" as Callie liked to call it, and was trying to decide on something to fix for dinner when Luke joined them in the kitchen, fresh from his shower.

He'd dressed in clean clothes, pulled no doubt from his saddlebags. He smelled of her hand-milled soap, and his still-damp hair curled over his shirt collar.

The color of his polo shirt made his eyes look as amazingly blue as the Arizona sky, and the fabric stretched over his chest emphasized its breadth and male muscularity.

His well-worn jeans hugged his legs like a second skin, delineating their shape and power. He'd tucked his feet into a pair of expensive-looking loafers. Only his bronzed tan made him look like he belonged here. Everything else about him laid claim to a far better life-style than the one she shared with Callie.

That reminder stole her breath and reduced her to a truth she couldn't escape. Luke would leave as soon as his repairs were made—and she and Callie would resume their own lives.

"I was just about to make dinner," she said, but Luke shook his head.

"The night's too hot to heat up the kitchen. How about I take you and Callie out for dinner?"

"There's no place that's really close—except the pizza place in town. Anything else would be a drive," she said.

"I happen to like pizza. How about you, princess?" he said to Callie.

"I love pizza. Can we go, Mommy? Please?"

Mariah knew there wasn't anything she could fix for dinner that would please her daughter now that Luke had mentioned pizza. She worried about Callie getting her vegetables, but she supposed going without them one night wouldn't hurt.

Besides, how could she crush the expectant look on her child's face?

Even Luke's face bore a hopeful look.

She knew when she was defeated.

"Okay," she said. "But then we'll come back here for dessert. I made a peach pie."

"Pizza, then homemade peach pie—I may never leave here."

But Mariah knew he *would,* probably sooner rather than later. And if she didn't want to hurt when he did, she needed to keep a tight rein on her emotions.

Also, there would be no more shared kisses in the moonlight—or on a picnic blanket, she reminded herself as she remembered *today's* lapse of judgment.

Mariah could be determined when she set her mind to it.

And the situation with Luke called for all the determination she could muster.

They pulled up in front of Rudy's Pizza, and Mariah parked the truck in front of the tin-roofed building. Sunrise was so small Luke wasn't sure how it even rated the designation of town. But he'd seen the city limit sign on the drive in, along with its proud mention that 239 people comprised its citizenry.

And Luke had the feeling Mariah knew every one of them.

At least it seemed that way as she spoke to Rudy and at least a dozen of the man's customers on the way in, all of whom had heard about Luke and his unlucky encounter with that disagreeable armadillo in the road.

He was definitely the center of attention, though he didn't want to be. He began to wish he hadn't suggested this outing and had stayed put at Mariah's, instead. The town, it seemed, had an overactive grapevine—one that could easily outrival the one at the trauma center back in Chicago.

That life now seemed a fantasy world, or a bad

dream. A nightmare. His life today, this moment, was far different. If he were in Chicago he'd be dining at some chic restaurant, probably on the waterfront or the Magnificent Mile.

Instead he was here at Rudy's with Mariah Cade, a woman more beautiful in her own special way than any woman he'd ever dined with before. And he liked that— with the possible exception that half the town was here, as well, every one of them staring at him.

Mariah introduced him, and for the next few minutes Luke had to field questions about his accident along with a few chuckles from the male customers about his city-boy blunder.

The women wanted to know more, like where he was from, how long he would be staying, and a few more…personal questions that Mariah neatly deflected.

She seemed to understand he'd be uncomfortable discussing a past that caused him pain—though she had no idea what his past was or anything about his pain. He hadn't shared that part of himself with her. But she had sensed—and respected—that privacy in him.

And Luke was grateful.

They finally escaped the group and found a table at the back.

Callie climbed onto her chair with an agility he had to marvel at. "Isn't this fun, Luke?" she asked him.

About as much fun as a sharp stick in the eye, he thought.

"Sure is, Callie."

He tried his best to sound enthusiastic as he took his seat next to Mariah. Damn, but she smelled good, her scent soft and soapy-clean and all feminine.

Her white shorts did little to hide her long, silky legs. The green top she wore brought out the color of her eyes. Her face was bronzed from the sun and free of makeup, letting her sheer beauty glow with its freshness. Only her lips carried a hint of man-made color, a soft, glossy shade of peach in the light of the restaurant.

"I'm sorry about all the scrutiny," she said when the buzz had finally quieted. "I guess I should have warned you. Small-town gossip can be horrific sometimes. And before you ask, I swear I didn't tell a soul about the armadillo."

Luke suspected the blame for that went to Una, or maybe Eli, who no doubt thought it fodder for the gossip mill. But he supposed he couldn't criticize them. It wasn't every day that a stranger on a motorcycle met misfortune trying to avoid an armor-plated critter in the road.

"I'm sure I'll live it down," he said. "Someday."

Callie giggled at his pique.

"I thought you were on my side, princess," he said with mock gruffness—which made her giggle all the more.

They put in their order for Rudy's largest pizza, which was covered with everything the proprietor could come up with, and soft drinks for the three of them.

"Rudy's pizza is good," Callie informed him.

"I sure hope so. I'm really hungry."

A waitress brought their drinks and when she'd left, Luke turned to Mariah. "Thanks for warding off some of the more personal questions," he said.

Mariah lowered her gaze. She *had* warded off some of the questions—for Luke's sake. She wasn't sure why. Or maybe she did know. It was because of what she read in his face, in his eyes, pain he wasn't ready to share, not with her.

And certainly not with a townful of strangers.

She took a sip of her drink, then glanced up at him. He looked like he was beginning to relax now that the citizenry of Sunrise had quit interrogating him.

"No thanks is necessary," she said.

He gave her a slow smile, and she noticed some of the shadows had left his eyes.

Callie leaned forward to tell him her favorite knock-knock joke, one Mariah had heard a dozen times. But Luke seemed to enjoy it, and laughed at the appropriate time.

Mariah liked his laugh, the deep timbre of it, the honesty of it, the way his eyes crinkled at the edges. She'd like to hear the sound more often, see the wonderful things it did to his face.

Luke was a handsome man.

Easily the most handsome she'd ever met.

Just then the waitress delivered the pizza to their table, interrupting Mariah's reverie, for which Mariah was grateful. She was spending far too much time thinking about the man sitting so close beside her.

"Mmm, *great* pizza," Luke said after he'd sampled a bite.

"I told you it was good," Callie said.

"You sure did, princess." He took another bite.

Mariah laughed at the look of pure rapture on his face. "Pretty good for Podunkville, huh?" she asked.

"Sunrise might be small," he said, "but it's far from being Podunkville."

Especially with a woman like Mariah in it, he thought.

He enjoyed watching her nibble at her slice of pizza, sipping her drink, dabbing her lips with her napkin. He needed to forget the feel of them under his, that sweet taste.

The woman was a temptation he didn't need.

"We don't have a cycle repair shop," she reminded him.

"Okay—one drawback," he said.

A major drawback, he thought. It would keep him here longer—and with Mariah's big green eyes and sexy smile, that could be dangerous. She set him on fire so easily. And he wasn't right for her—not for any woman—right now.

"Oops!" Mariah bent her head and took a sip of her drink.

"Oops, what?" he asked, glancing around. New customers had filed into the place. In fact, he had the feeling it was the other half of the population—all here to take a look at the new man in town. "I'm being scrutinized again?"

"'Fraid so."

Luke wiped pizza from his mouth. He felt like a sideshow. "Are people around here always this curious?" he asked.

"Anyone new in town gets grilled, I'm afraid. But they may be a little more ruthless than usual with you because…"

"Because why?"

She hesitated. "Because they're probably thinking that you…we…"

He raised an eyebrow. "Are an item?"

She nodded.

An ugly thought crossed his mind. "Mariah, is my

staying at your place causing you problems with the town?"

"You mean, is my reputation on the griddle?"

"If it is—"

"It isn't. It's just that…well, they're probably just hoping that there's something between us. They'd like to see me married, with some man looking after me."

He was quiet for a moment as she sipped her drink. Damn, now how had he waded into this? Mariah hardly needed a man to look after her; she could take care of herself and Callie on her own. But any man worth his salt would *want* to take care of her.

And Luke had proved he couldn't take care of anyone.

"What's rep-tation?" Callie wanted to know, her small face tilted up to her mother's.

"It…it's nothing, sweetheart," she said to Callie. "Just big-people talk."

"Oh."

Mariah gave him a warning glance.

Luke nodded.

The last thing he wanted was to bring trouble to this small, special family.

Callie fell asleep on the ride home, and when they reached the house, Luke carried her inside and laid her on the bed among her tumble of stuffed animals.

"Thank you," Mariah whispered to him, then turned to get her daughter into a freshly washed nightie without waking her.

Fortunately Callie stayed asleep.

Mariah drew up the covers, then as she often did, spent a quiet moment looking down at her sweet child, so very glad that she had her—and wishing with a mother's heart that she could hold Callie's disease at bay.

It had already taken its toll on her young joints, but Mariah was determined to minimize her daughter's disability as much as she was able.

She wanted so much for Callie, wanted her to grow up sure and confident, strong and capable—capable of tackling the world with all its traps and pitfalls.

She didn't kid herself about Callie's illness, or how difficult life could be for her, but her daughter had spunk; she didn't allow herself to be hampered by braces or her illness.

Callie would do well.

But still, Mariah worried.

She wished she had that one magic herb, root or plant that could wipe away this cruel disease. But she didn't have a cure—and as a mother, that saddened her.

She gave a deep sigh and kissed Callie on the forehead, placed one of her favorite stuffed animals beside her, then silently slipped from the room.

Mariah wondered if Luke had left, retreated to the cabin out behind. Then she heard the creak of the porch swing, a restful, and somehow intimate, sound in the quiet of the night.

She'd promised the man peach pie, she remembered.

She headed toward the kitchen and the pie she'd left cooling on the windowsill. Taking it down, she cut a large slice for Luke and a smaller one for herself. Grabbing some napkins and two forks, she carried everything out to the porch to join Luke.

"Did you get Callie down all right?" he asked, stopping the to and fro motion of the swing.

"She didn't even wake. She really enjoyed herself tonight," she said, handing him his plate.

His eyes lit up at the sight of the dessert. "I was hoping you'd remember the peach pie. My mouth has been watering for it ever since we got back," he said.

She smiled and took a seat on the top porch step, careful to keep a sane distance from this man who could rattle her senses with very little provocation.

His male scent mingled with the night and the moonlight—and did dangerous things to her senses. Moonlight and Luke didn't mix well for her. She remembered last night in front of the cabin and the kiss they'd shared beneath this very same moon. She swallowed hard and struggled to get her thoughts in check.

She didn't need a repeat of last night—or this afternoon, either, for that matter.

"Mmm, this is great pie," he said. "Even better than my grandmother used to make. And believe me, that's a compliment. Grams was a whiz in the kitchen."

Mariah was pleased with his praise. "So, your grandmother, did she spoil you?"

He gave a grin. "Spoil me? Of course—I was her only grandson."

He said it without a shred of shame, and Mariah had to smile.

"Tell me about your family," she said, hoping it wouldn't make him retreat behind that shadow of pain she too often saw in his eyes.

All she knew about him was that he came from Chicago, a man on his way to nowhere, a man with a wounded soul.

"What can I say?" He gave a shrug of his wide shoulders. "I grew up in a typical family, more or less. Maybe a little richer than some. And I admit I was spoiled, obnoxiously so."

"By your grandmother and her peach pie?"

A corner of his mouth lifted in a smile. "Yeah, but my mother did her share, too."

"A mother can never love a child too much," she said, thinking of Callie, of how much she was a part of Mariah's heart.

"Okay, I was *loved* to the point of being spoiled. Is that better?"

She gave a slight smile. "A *little* better."

"My dad was rough on me, though. Of course, I probably deserved it," he added with a devilish grin.

"Were you a wild child?"

He took another bite of his pie, then swallowed. "I was sweet and lovable. Still am."

His answer made her laugh. Or maybe it was the indignant expression he flashed at her.

He finished the last piece of his pie, then eyed her plate. "Aren't you going to eat yours?"

Mariah hadn't touched it—and she wasn't sure she wanted it after all. Maybe it was thinking about what was to come, Luke riding off to somewhere, never seeing him again.

After he'd tempted her heart.

"I'm not really hungry," she said. "Do you want it?"

"If you're not going to eat it…"

"I'm still full from dinner, really." It wasn't a complete lie. She'd had several large slices of pizza, more than her usual. She handed him the plate.

A smile curved at his lips, and Mariah tried not to

notice what it did to his face, softening it, lessening the heartbreak she knew was there within him, the heartbreak he tried so hard to hide.

"Thank you," he said.

"Thank *you*," she countered. "For tonight. For dinner. I enjoyed it."

His gaze remained on her for a long moment and her heart thudded against the backside of her ribs.

"Mariah, it was the least I could do to repay you for letting me stay here."

She lowered her gaze from his and drew a deep breath. Luke saw this thing between them as nothing more than simple hospitality. And she should, as well. What was wrong with her? Did she need a man that much?

Two days ago she'd have answered with a resounding "no," but that was before Luke had happened into her life and made her feel as uncertain as a schoolgirl.

He cut into her slice of pie—a man-size bite.

There was nothing dainty about Luke Phillips.

Watching him eat, watching him do most *anything* fascinated her, but it was a fascination she shouldn't get too used to. Luke wasn't part of her life.

Nor would he be.

Where was he headed—and why? What was the pain she saw in his eyes? Had someone betrayed him, the way Will had betrayed her and Callie?

What would make him whole again? The right woman? A place? Wherever the place was, it wasn't Sunrise.

And she wasn't the woman.

Luke would be leaving soon. The way Will had left. Luke might not be the same kind of man, but he didn't belong here, any more than she belonged in his world.

He finished her piece of pie, too, and stood up to take the plates to the kitchen.

"I can do that," she said and reached for them.

"Mariah," he said solemnly. "I enjoyed tonight."

His voice was so low, so soft, she wasn't sure she heard him.

"Me, too," she answered. "Very much."

She feared he might kiss her, feared she might let him. She clutched the plates closer. "I—I really should go in. It's…getting late."

He nodded, and Mariah started for the door.

"Good night, Luke."

"Good night," he said.

She left him standing there in the moonlight, on her porch—before she did something foolish.

Something that would put her heart in peril.

Luke tossed and turned half the night. He knew every knothole in the wood that made up the cabin's ceiling and walls. He recognized every sound from without: the yip of the coyotes, a truck rumbling down the graveled road to somewhere, the sough of the wind through the cottonwood tree outside.

The moonlight slipped into the cabin through the small window and the tiny chinks between the logs. This place wouldn't be warm in winter, he thought.

Where would he be come winter?

Sunning himself on a sandy California beach? Or still riding his cycle to nowhere in search of peace for his damned soul?

Luke couldn't think that far ahead.

He had to take life one day at a time, fighting his

demons and hoping that one day he could forgive himself for his failure. One thing he knew for certain— he'd never go anywhere even remotely close to a hospital again.

The practice of medicine held too many memories, too much anguish, too much pain.

Mariah had helped him forget his misery for this short while—and for that he'd be forever in her debt. She asked few questions of him, yet she seemed to understand he was hurting and wasn't ready to talk about it yet.

She was in tune with the world, sensed everything about the people who came into her life—even briefly. Empathy. He'd never known anyone to whom it came so naturally.

It was what made her a healer.

Too bad he wasn't one she could heal.

At two in the morning his eyelids became heavy. He could get in a few good hours of sleep—if visions of Mariah didn't haunt him, if her soft scent didn't tease at his senses.

If his libido didn't damn him yet another night.

Mariah strapped the seat belt around Callie and climbed into the passenger seat of her ancient truck. It used to be white, but had long ago faded to an uninspiring cream. But she was just grateful she had transportation of any sort.

She wasn't a woman who was hard to please. If someone handed her keys to a new Mercedes she wouldn't know what to do with them. She knew her truck inside out—with all its balky foibles.

Callie was looking forward to the drive to Cottonwood. She'd insisted on wearing her pink sundress with a splash of white daisies and green leaves embroidered along the hem. The flowered border made the braces on her thin legs less apparent, though Callie's disability could in no way detract from the child's soft beauty.

She smelled of soap and little girl. Her dark hair was pinned back with her favorite barrette. The smile on her face attested to her excitement over their day's excursion.

Mariah was torn about the trip. She was looking forward to spending the day with Luke, but she knew that once he had the part he needed for his cycle, there would no longer be any need for him to stay around.

"Are we ready?" he asked as he joined them, sliding in behind the wheel.

"Uh-huh," Callie said. "We're going on a trip."

"A trip?" Luke remarked. "Just how far is Cottonwood, anyway?"

"Not far," Mariah said. "About forty miles."

Luke's gaze lingered on her, sliding over her scoop-necked red top where just the hint of cleavage showed. Maybe she should have worn something else, she thought—something with a higher neckline. But this went with her red-striped denim Capri pants and showed off her Indian-beaded dangly earrings to advantage.

But Luke wasn't noticing earrings—and suddenly Mariah felt uneasy. She'd never dressed to tease, but today it certainly felt like she was out for attention.

Luke's attention.

She squirmed a bit in her seat.

"Forty miles—that should be a snap," he said and finally took his eyes off her, and started up the old truck.

"You should reserve judgment about that until you see the road we have to take," she said.

This time his gaze settled on her lips. She'd only added a touch of lip gloss. It was the only makeup she wore. Nervously she licked her lower lip.

"I take it we're not traveling the interstate?" he said, his gaze disconnecting from her mouth to the rearview mirror as he backed the truck out of Mariah's long, winding driveway.

"There's no interstate between here and Cottonwood, I'm afraid."

"Terrific—that means we should be there in…what…three days? If we're lucky?"

Mariah wasn't sure if he was kidding—or cursing the harsh landscape. She forgot he came from a big city and wasn't used to these backcountry roads. Nor was he used to driving an old truck, she thought, as the engine sputtered.

His gaze shot to her, a nervous crease in his forehead.

"Don't worry—the truck is fine. It just…makes noises sometimes."

"Makes noises…"

That wasn't exactly a mechanical turn of phrase, but she knew her truck. It would get them there.

And back.

"Did we get up on the wrong side of the bed this morning?" she asked a bit sharply.

His gaze slid to hers, and for a moment, he said nothing, then his face bore a look of apology. "I'm sorry. Am I being a bear today?" he asked.

"A minor bear."

He let out a deep laugh at that. "Bad enough that you'd leave me in the desert and drive off?"

She pretended to consider the prospect. "We'll see how it goes."

He gave a quick glance around at the barren landscape. "I'll mend my ways."

She smiled. "Sounds like a start."

"Actually it was Bandit's fault," he said. "He was my wake-up call again this morning. Does that crazy bird ever take a vacation?"

Mariah laughed. "'Fraid not."

Luke did well driving the truck, taking the curves in stride and propelling the machine over the rutted gravel road with a minimum of jolts.

Which was better for Callie's joints.

Was Luke taking her daughter's condition into consideration?

As he averted another small groove in the road, Mariah realized he was doing just that. Even if it meant getting to Cottonwood later than he'd like.

"Are we going to get ice cream when we get there?" Callie asked.

Luke took a quick glance at his watch. "We'd better have lunch first, princess. Then we'll think about that ice cream."

"I like lunch, too," Callie informed him.

Luke gave her daughter a gentle smile.

He looked handsome today—as handsome as they came, she thought as her gaze drifted over him, from his sun-streaked brown hair, his smiling blue eyes, that sexy mouth she remembered kissing, to his mountain-wide shoulders in that black knit shirt that set off his tan to perfection.

Yes, the man was handsome all right. His presence seemed to fill the cab of her small truck. His broad hands rested easily on the wheel, hands that had brushed her cheek, sending jolts of electricity through her. His smile was dynamite. She enjoyed seeing it—and wished he'd use it more often.

And his kiss…

Mariah needed to forget the feel of his lips on hers.

They were kisses that would take them nowhere—except into trouble. Trouble Mariah didn't need. And, she suspected, neither did Luke.

Chapter Seven

Luke pulled into a parking spot in front of the bike shop and climbed out of the truck.

"I won't be long," he said. "Then we'll find a place to have lunch."

"And ice cream," Callie reminded.

Luke gave her a smile, unable to resist the little girl for long. "And ice cream," he promised her.

He hadn't started out the morning on a very good note. His crazy thoughts about Mariah had finally allowed him to fall asleep, only to have Bandit's caterwauling awaken him a few hours later.

But whatever the cause of his prickly mood, Mariah had taken him to task for it. She was no flower wilting in the desert. She was as tough as an Arizona cactus—at least when it came to determination.

In every other way, though, she was as soft and

feminine as any man could want. And that was Luke's problem.

He *wanted* Mariah.

His body was strung as tight as a bowstring and his nerves were beginning to fray around the edges. Mariah was all too tempting—and Luke was on a short tether.

"Can I help you, sir?"

Luke shot a glance at the clerk behind the counter as if he was about to be his salvation. "I hope so." He handed over the damaged brake part. "I need one of these."

In the worst way, Luke wanted to add.

The guy examined the metal piece. "Lemme check our stock," he said.

He took off to the back room, and Luke let out a slow sigh. Maybe he'd have his bike operational by this time tomorrow—with a little luck and Eli's help.

While he waited he checked out the display of bike accessories, but nothing tempted his wallet. He gave a glance out the front window and saw Mariah and Callie. Mariah was laughing at something her daughter had said, her mouth curved in delight.

Luke had tasted that mouth, knew its every corner and contour, how it felt beneath his—a whisper of silk, a sultry promise that could threaten a man's sanity.

Just then the clerk returned, pulling Luke's thoughts back to business.

"Sorry, buddy," he said. "I don't have the part you need."

"You sure?" Luke asked.

"I'm sure."

Luke gave a quiet curse. "Do you happen to know where I might find one? It's important."

The guy frowned—and Luke had the feeling he'd heard the "important" line before.

"Closest place would be Phoenix."

This time Luke frowned. "There's no place closer?"

"Nope."

Luke wasn't about to drive all the way to Phoenix and subject Callie to the long trip. Just the ride to this place had probably done damage to her fragile joints.

But Callie had wanted to come along. Those green eyes, so like her pretty mother's, had lit at the prospect.

"I can order the part," the clerk offered.

"Order." Why hadn't the guy said that sooner? "How long will that take?"

"Should be in early next week—Tuesday, most likely."

Luke did the math—five days. He didn't like it, but it would have to do. "Okay," he said. "Order it for me—I'll be back Tuesday to pick it up."

His mood was back to irritable as he headed out of the shop. He'd have to find some way to resist Mariah for a few more days.

Five days.

And that, he knew, would be a challenge.

Mariah glanced toward the store as Luke came out. He looked about as happy as a man facing a root canal. He opened the truck door and slid in behind the wheel.

"What's wrong?" she asked.

He slammed the truck door. "The part needs to be ordered—won't be in until Tuesday."

Mariah knew she should feel disappointed, but she was unable to summon up the emotion. Luke would be here longer—and if nothing else, that would be a benefit to his injuries. They would have a little more time to heal.

"Well, that's not exactly the end of the world. Tuesday will come—next week. It follows Monday."

"Very funny," he returned.

Callie giggled at that, which seemed to bring him around a little. He gave a small smile. It wasn't much, but it was better than nothing, she supposed.

"I'm being a bear again," he said.

"I'm glad I don't have to point that out."

He started up the truck. "Sorry—maybe lunch will improve my mood."

"And ice cream," Callie added.

This time he dug up a full smile, a handsome one, she had to admit. "Right," he said. "But lunch first, small fry."

They found a café on the way out of town, a family-type place with roomy red booths. Callie wanted Luke to sit next to her and tugged at his sleeve to pull him down beside her.

Mariah took a seat across from them.

Callie was getting attached to the man—and that worried Mariah. He wouldn't be staying—and she wasn't sure Callie really understood that.

Little girls needed a male influence in their lives; she knew that. Mariah had grown up without *her* father. She hadn't even known him. Nor did she want to. She had nothing but antipathy for a man who would run away from his responsibilities, especially responsibilities to a child.

Mariah had always tried to make it up to Callie for her lack of a father, hoping her daughter wouldn't grow up scarred by what was clearly Will's failing.

Luke was reading the menu to Callie, and her

daughter's eyes lit up at everything he reeled off. At home Mariah made sure Callie ate healthy, but she wouldn't have a chance of talking her into something healthy today.

Not with Luke as her culprit-in-crime.

Maybe she'd indulge in something sinful herself. But the most sinful thing wasn't on the menu, she thought. He was seated across the table from her.

Luke Phillips.

A man who'd ridden into her life one warm, sunny day—and would ride out of it just as certainly.

"A penny for your thoughts," he said, his gaze sliding over her and making her skin tingle.

"Just deciding what looks good," she said, then opened her menu.

He raised an eyebrow. "See anything you want?"

She felt a warm blush stain her cheeks. Why had she said that? Because Luke had caught her gaping at him and read her mind, that's why.

And her mind wasn't on lunch.

She lowered her gaze, not good at playing games, games she shouldn't have started in the first place. She didn't need Luke knowing she was attracted to him, that her senses flared just looking at him, that his touch, his kiss, made her giddy, that she was…

A fool.

She closed her menu and gave him a brave smile. "A burger and fries," she said.

The waitress appeared, and he tore his gaze away from her and gave their order. He made his a double *everything,* and Mariah wondered where he stored all those calories.

His stomach was flat and lean. She remembered him yesterday without his shirt—and her body temperature rose a few uncomfortable degrees. She took a sip of the water the waitress had brought, hoping to cool her sensibilities.

What was it about this man that had her forgetting who she was? A mother with a child. A woman who needed to remember men didn't stay around in her life.

There, that should bring her back to much-needed reality.

It didn't take long for their food to arrive. Callie looked enthralled with her adult-size burger, and had fun dipping her fries in catsup like Luke was doing.

She chattered away to him, no doubt boring the man to death. But he didn't appear to mind her talkativeness.

Occasionally his gaze strayed across the table to Mariah—and each time it did, her body reacted. It was that smile, the way his mouth curved at the edges, as if he were sharing some private amusement with her.

That dark shadow of pain she too often read in his eyes had retreated to some inner place for now—and Mariah hoped that this casual day had temporarily eased his demons.

Luke ordered ice cream for Callie and some for himself, but Mariah didn't indulge. She could stretch her decadence only so far in one day. That was a good point to remember the next time her lips begged to be kissed.

But there wasn't going to be a next time. Mariah had endangered her senses enough. She couldn't risk more temptation.

"I'm sorry our trip turned out to be a wild-goose chase," he said, glancing across the table at her again. "I thought I'd have the cycle back together by tomorrow for sure."

The best-laid plans, Mariah thought. He had a small

dab of chocolate beside his mouth, and she wanted to reach over and wipe it away. Or maybe she just wanted to touch him. Fortunately he dabbed it with his napkin before she could do anything that foolish.

"So it will take a little longer to get your bike up and running. Your war wounds will appreciate the rest."

"My war wounds are in good shape, Mariah."

She'd seen his injuries. They weren't healed any more than the pain in his heart was healed. Unfortunately her herbs couldn't do much for that kind of pain.

Nor could he outrun it with his cycle.

She wanted to tell him that—but it was a realization he needed to come to himself.

"I think I'd better take a look at them, despite your say-so. You can think of it as a second opinion."

Mariah wasn't sure, but she thought she saw him turn a little green.

"We're home, sweetheart," Mariah said and unbuckled her seat belt, then Callie's. Her daughter had fallen asleep soon after they were back in the truck.

Luke had gotten the ancient AM radio to work, something that surprised Mariah. The thing hadn't worked for years and she'd considered it hopeless.

But with Luke's well-positioned thump, it had come to life.

She and Luke had sung along with some of the tunes, despite the scratchy transmission. He sang well, his voice a deep baritone. Mariah was a little off-key, but thankfully he didn't point that out.

They were tired, but it was a nice tired. Mariah only hoped Callie didn't suffer any ill effects.

Luke lifted her daughter to the ground, making sure she was steady on her braces before he released her. Mariah was surprised at his seeming knowledge of Callie's illness.

That made her curious.

"I had fun today, Luke," Callie said when she was balanced on her awkward braces. Her voice was still sleepy, her pretty sundress wrinkled from her nap, a small blotch of chocolate ice cream decorating the front of it.

"I had fun too, princess."

"Can we go again soon?"

He laughed at that. "Not too soon, I hope. I think we should rest up from today."

Callie gave a small nod at that.

Mariah wished Luke wouldn't offer promises to Callie, even vague promises like this one. Callie would be disappointed if something came up and she couldn't go when the next time came.

She remembered the promises Will had made.

Promises not kept.

Callie glanced up at Luke. "Is my mommy gonna fix your leg now?"

Luke gave a low groan that sounded more like a growl. "She thinks she is, but my leg is just fine."

Mariah turned to him. "I *am* going to look at that leg as well as your other scrapes and bruises."

"I think she means it," Callie whispered to Luke as he steadied her again when they reached the porch steps.

"Think so?"

"Mmm-hmm. I know when she means something and when she doesn't."

"Is that right?" Mariah hid a smile. "You must think you're one smart little girl."

"I *am* smart," Callie insisted.

Mariah ushered her daughter into her bedroom, then turned back to Luke. "Don't go anywhere," she warned. "As soon as I get Callie down for her nap, I'm going to have a look at that leg."

He gave a frown as she ushered Callie into her bedroom.

Luke knew he could escape to the cabin, but the stubborn woman would just come after him. Instead he headed for the kitchen and a slice of Mariah's peach pie. He wasn't all that hungry, not after a huge lunch, but Mariah made the very best peach pie he'd ever tasted.

And where on his long road to nowhere would he find homemade peach pie?

He'd just finished his last bite when Mariah entered the kitchen. He carried his plate and fork to the sink. "Had to have another slice," he said. "It's so delicious."

She smiled at the compliment. "I'm glad you enjoyed it."

"Did you get Callie to sleep?"

"No," she said. "But she agreed to a little quiet time with her books and dolls. That will have to do. She's still excited about her day."

"I hope the trip wasn't too much for her."

"I do, too. At any rate, when the part comes in, I think you should take the truck and go by yourself. It's a pretty full day when we go to Cottonwood so we don't do it often."

"I understand. And I appreciate the loan of the truck."

Luke could never repay Mariah for all she'd done for him, but he'd never forget her generosity. Nor would he be able to forget her.

No matter how hard he tried.

"Now it's time to take a look at those cuts and bruises. Undress. There's a towel in the cabinet."

She motioned him into the room off her kitchen. But Luke stood his ground.

"You don't need to look at them. They're doing just fine."

"And you're an expert?"

Actually he was. He was still enough of a doctor to know that his injuries were superficial and would heal eventually. What he wasn't as sure of was whether he could survive Mariah's sweet hands on him a second time.

"Look, Mariah—" he began, then shut his mouth on a groan.

He might as well save his breath. Mariah wasn't listening anyway. She was busy pulling herbs from her cabinet, along with an old-fashioned mortar and pestle.

"On the drive back I remembered a special mixture I've made in the past," she said. "It will speed up the healing if you're so all-fired determined to get back on that bike of yours."

"I'm determined."

"Fine—then get those clothes off."

Luke gave another groan. He'd walked directly into that one.

Luke was the most stubborn man Mariah had ever met. Too bad there wasn't an herb to cure that, she thought as she gathered up her supplies and headed for the treatment room—and her patient.

Patient was the operative word here.

Luke was just another patient, nothing more. She raised her chin, determined to remember that.

She found him pacing the small room, a white towel wrapped around his middle. Her raised chin lost a whole lot of that determination at the sight of him and his sculpted muscles.

This was your idea, Mariah, she reminded herself. *Now, deal with it.*

She forced herself to take a breath and willed her heart to still its thunderous pace.

"I need you to sit here," she told him and motioned him to the chair beside her worktable.

He glanced at the small tray holding her supplies, then at her. He didn't look any more excited about this than she did. And Mariah couldn't say she blamed him.

How had she thought she could think of him as just another patient when everything about Luke Phillips made her edgy? She knew the feel of those muscles.

"Sit," she said again.

Luke gave a fierce scowl, but reluctantly took a seat and stretched his long legs out in front of him. "Might as well get this over with," he said.

Mariah swallowed hard and reined in her emotions. She'd never had a patient as totally male as Luke—but she was a healer. She had the skills Una had so patiently taught her. She knew her herbs and medicinals.

She drew in a breath and adjusted her treatment light to illuminate the injury on his shoulder. Actually it looked much improved from the other day.

"This is healing nicely," she said.

"Told you, but you didn't want to listen."

She frowned at him. "You didn't let me finish. I was about to say, the bruise beneath it looks awful."

"Awful? Is that a medical term?"

Luke knew it wasn't, but he couldn't resist a little ribbing. To take his mind off the woman in front of him.

She drew back and gave him a glower. "Do you ever allow anyone to help you, Luke Phillips?"

Luke didn't need help. He could take care of himself. Just not now, with the thought of Mariah's sensual hands so close.

"Not often," he said.

She gave an exasperated sigh. "Then get used to the experience."

Just what he needed—a determined healer.

She probed the bruise with gentle fingers. It was a little tender but that was to be expected after the fall he'd taken. He'd survived a lot worse pain in his life, was still enduring a pain for which there was no relief.

Mariah poured some of her herbal mixture into the palm of her hand then applied it to the bruise on his shoulder. The oil was warm, sensual. And she made it even more so, with the way her fingers massaged, working their magic.

"What is this stuff—snake oil?" he asked.

"Oil of armadillo."

The quip rolled easily off her lips—and despite himself, Luke had to laugh. He tried to relax under her touch, her fingers stroking, kneading, lacing the heat into the deep recesses of the bruise.

"Seriously," he said. "What is it?"

"Birch bark, borage—and a few other plant parts, all heated in *pinon* oil. The heat of my hand helps the compound penetrate into the bruised tissue."

She found his other bruises and repeated her massage, her hands skillful, adept—and for one dangerous moment he wondered what they'd feel like on other parts of his body.

No, he couldn't, *wouldn't,* go there—despite the fact that his body felt the sweet ache, the longing to mate with her, feel her heat.

He clenched his jaw, marshalling his defenses.

When she'd finished massaging away the pain in his shoulder and other upper bruises, she turned to the gash on his thigh.

"That one's fine," he lied.

How could he let those sultry hands touch him there? His libido was on a short fuse already; that could only make it worse.

"Good, then it won't need much attention. Now—let me see it."

She stood her ground, not giving a visible inch.

Luke's groan was low, guttural. If she massaged that oil on his thigh he'd have her on her back on that worktable in a quick Chicago minute.

And he couldn't be responsible for what happened.

Even without the massage, it was a possibility waiting to happen. Mariah was a sexy, sensual woman. And Luke was bothered.

She waited patiently.

"Okay, okay," he said finally. "I suppose you won't be happy until you have a look."

He slid the towel up a modest inch—but at least she

could view the cut. It had hurt like hell all day. But he didn't intend to tell her that.

And, admittedly, he should have cleansed and dressed it better. As a doctor he knew that—but he didn't give a lot of attention to his needs these days.

He plain didn't care about his own misery.

Her fingers touched the edges of the cut, gently pinching them together, approximating sutures. "I probably should have insisted you get this stitched," she said.

"It didn't need stitches. And it's healing just fine."

She worked to clean the wound with something that burned like fire. She hadn't offered him that bullet to bite on this time—and he could use it.

"It'll heal with a ragged scar," she said. "But I'll see what I can do."

Luke just hoped whatever "she could do" she'd do fast.

He wanted to get this over with.

She searched around in her supply cabinet for something. Forceps, he saw. Then she bent down on one knee and carefully plucked something from the open wound.

"Denim—from your jeans. Not exactly germ-free. Why didn't you keep it dressed?"

"Didn't have time. I was busy trying to get the cycle fixed."

Her gaze met his, and he saw major annoyance in her eyes. "Even though you shouldn't ride it anyway."

Luke heard the sharp edge in her voice—and he couldn't blame her. If one of his patients had taken care of a wound like Luke had taken care of his, he'd have had an edge to his tone, too.

He struggled with an apology. "I know, Mariah. You did a good job, patching me up, then I…I blew it. I'm sorry."

"You should be sorry." She stood and rummaged in her supplies again. "I'm not sure what I can do—but I'll do the best I can."

And she would, Luke knew. She always did her best, no matter what it was—or how important. Her patients were lucky to have her—and he hoped they appreciated her work.

Better than he had.

She turned back to him with something crushed and purple in color. "What's that stuff?" he asked.

"Lavender powder with a few other herbs mixed in," she answered and sprinkled some of it into the cleansed wound on his thigh.

It soothed the raw gash, and Luke felt himself relax a little as she worked.

Her hair hung loose, flowing sensually down her back, so inviting, so silken, he wanted to touch it. Her shoulders were narrow, but Luke knew they carried a hidden strength, a strength he had to admire.

Her medical instincts were good—and he'd bet she could cure an elephant of a head cold if she tried. Her ministrations today had eased his pain and helped his wounds.

He'd resisted for only one reason: her hands.

They drove him wild.

He concentrated on how she was pulling the jagged edges of the gash together and taping them with Steri-Strips as facilely as any E.R. doc he knew.

"There," she said, finishing up. "Now all it needs is a dressing. And a man who'll take care of it, instead of ripping it open working on his bike."

She sent him a daggered look.

And Luke was ready to promise her anything.

She placed several squares of gauze over the cut and taped it to his leg, then drew back to admire her handiwork.

"Thank you," he said.

"It was nothing."

Her voice was low and sweet, a velvet whisper in the small room. And Luke's resolve developed a major crack. Her lips were close, too close—and he had to taste them. Had to know if they tasted as sultry as they looked at that moment. He lowered his mouth to hers. Just a taste, he'd promised himself.

Just a taste.

Her lips were fire and temptation, and Luke felt the last of his resolve shatter like a plate glass window. He drew her up against him, felt her slight hesitation at first, or maybe it was surprise. Whichever, it soon gave way to soft surrender.

She gave a small moan of need, and Luke knew he was damned. He deepened the kiss, taking the sound into him, absorbing it the way he absorbed her kiss and her body pressed so tantalizingly against his.

This time the moan was his.

Mariah knew she shouldn't be doing this—and in a minute she'd put a stop to it. His kiss felt too wonderful, too glorious to stop right now. She'd wanted this all day, she realized, no matter how hard her head tried to deny it.

Only the thin towel lay between them, not much of a barrier—especially if the towel came loose. But she didn't dare think of that.

Her imagination was fired up enough.

His mouth was lethal, moving slowly, languidly, over

hers as if he had all day. And night. Oh, how would it feel to lie beside him all night, her body sated by him time after time? How would it feel to wake up in his arms when morning arrived?

She hadn't experienced any times like that since Will had left, and even when he was here, it had never matched the thoughts she had of sharing nights with Luke.

Or mornings.

Luke was so much more than any man. She knew that. A man impossible to resist. No matter how much she knew she should.

Luke drew back and smiled down at her. Mariah was one glorious woman—and he never wanted to let her go. He traced her top lip with the tip of his tongue, outlining its shape, drinking in its nectar, then her lower one, so full, so perfect, and felt his body tighten, a sweet, torturous ache he knew only Mariah could satisfy.

He wanted her under him, wanted to make her beg for the same release *he* so desperately needed. "I want you so much," he whispered against her lips. "But I think we'd better stop this before it's too late."

"Mmm-hmm," she said. Her answer was muffled by his lips, but he took it as a yes.

Just one more kiss, one more taste, then he'd stop. But before Luke could steal that kiss, there was a knock on the back screen door.

Mariah jerked away as if she'd been caught with her hand in the cookie jar, then smoothed back her hair and went to the door while Luke pulled on his jeans.

"Hi, Eli," he heard her say.

Luke gave a sigh and decided that perhaps he owed

the kid a thank-you for his timing. What would have happened had this thing with Mariah gone on longer?

He went to the back door and stood beside her. "Hi, champ, what's up?"

"I came to see if you got the new part for the Harley."

"I'm afraid it'll have to wait until next week," Luke said. "The shop has to order in the part."

"Oh." Eli was clearly disappointed.

"But I can use your help then," Luke added. "If you're free."

The kid's face brightened. "Yeah," he answered. "I'll help." Then he bounded off the back porch and over to his grandmother's house.

"Great timing," Mariah said.

He drew a finger down her cheek, then brushed it over those tempting lips. "It's all in how you look at it."

Chapter Eight

After Luke left, Mariah went to gather up her things and put the small treatment room in order. His kiss had scattered her senses. All she could think about was the feel of his mouth on hers and the sparks still zinging through her body like so many fiery jolts of electricity.

What had happened to her focus?

Luke was a compelling man and she doubted she'd ever be able to eradicate him from her mind. He'd still be there in her life, hauntingly present, long after he'd ridden away on his cycle.

She'd always been able to lose herself in her herbs and her healings, always hoping for that one special plant that might cure her daughter.

Callie was her life, her reason to greet the sun in the morning, the reason the moon shone at night. She couldn't forget that, couldn't allow herself to find comfort in a man's arms—especially a man who wouldn't be around to share her life.

If Eli hadn't shown up when he had, what might have happened between them?

Mariah had the sensation of being on a freight train, racing toward the end of the track—and certain disaster. She couldn't let that happen. Callie didn't need a train wreck for a mother. She needed one who'd be there for her, preferably with brain intact.

Putting thoughts of Luke from her mind, she headed for the kitchen. Callie would be awake and hungry soon, despite the large lunch they'd had.

An hour later she had tortilla soup simmering on the stove and went to check on Callie. Her daughter had been quiet, and Mariah hoped she'd drifted off to sleep after all. With their trip today, she could use the rest.

Mariah knew something was wrong the moment she saw her.

Callie's eyes were bright and shiny with pain, pain Mariah had seen in them too many times before, and her little face was flushed with fever. She'd slept fitfully, the tangled bed covers testimony to that.

"I hurt, Mommy," she said, rubbing at her thin legs.

Mariah knew right away that their trip over the rough roads today had done damage to Callie's joints, made her illness flare to ugly life. She wanted to rail at the world, a world that could do this to a small child.

She took Callie into her arms, though she couldn't even hug her without hurting her more. Another cruelty. When Callie most needed to be embraced, held tight in her mother's arms, Mariah had to temper her touch. She smoothed back her daughter's hair, which was damp with fever, the same fever Mariah knew was in her hot, painful joints.

"I know, sweetheart," she said. "Mommy will try to make you feel better with her medicine."

It was a promise she hoped she could fulfill as she gently held her daughter. She wanted to absorb Callie's pain, take the ravages of it into her own body.

Her mind raced ahead to the herbs she could use. Gum weed for the inflammation. Some groundsel and dandelion root. She'd add them to the warm compresses for Callie's tender joints.

Then later, if Callie could bear it, she'd make up a heated herbal bath for her. Ground sunflower and the warm water always helped, but sometimes getting in and out of the tub was more pain than Callie could tolerate.

She planted a soft kiss on her daughter's feverish forehead and eased her back against the pillows. "You rest, sweetheart, while I go make up the warm packs."

She offered Callie a smile, a smile she didn't fully feel—not deep in her heart. Her native medicines could only ease her daughter's symptoms, not effect a cure.

Not that the doctors in Phoenix could do more.

She'd taken Callie to their clinics, their hospitals, but all their medicines had failed to work any better.

"What's wrong?"

Mariah wheeled around at the sound of the deep male voice behind her. Luke stood there in the doorway. He looked so tall, so strong—and for one weak moment she wanted to run to him, have him hold her, absorb some of his strength, a strength she could use right now.

Before she could speak, his keen gaze swept over

Callie. She saw in his eyes the moment he made the quick assessment: Callie was in trouble.

He went to her and sat on the edge of the bed, careful not to jostle her. His broad, gentle hand touched her forehead. "You're hot, princess."

"Uh-huh," Callie answered, sniffing back unshed tears. "And I hurt."

"I know, sweetie, I know—and I'm sorry." His voice was low and gentle, its very tone therapeutic.

He reached for Callie's knees, checking for heat in her painful joints, the way Mariah often did, the way the doctors had done. He did the same with her hips, her ankles, her wrists, her elbows and shoulders—and Mariah gasped.

"You…you do that like a doctor," she said.

Only then did he seem to remember that she was in the room. He turned to glance at her—and Mariah knew she hadn't imagined what she saw.

Luke *was* a doctor.

Why hadn't he told her? Why had he kept quiet about something that important? Why had he let her treat his wounds and not said a word?

Betrayal stabbed through her, sharp and quick. How primitive he must have found her medicines. She could imagine the amusement it must have given him.

"Are you, Luke? Are you…a doctor?"

Would he deny it?

His forehead creased. A muscle jumped along his jawline. The shadows she'd seen in his eyes haunted him again.

His voice, when it came, was low, agonized.

"I *was* a doctor."

* * *

Luke escaped outside, but he wasn't able to escape the past.

Images of himself in green scrubs played out before his eyes. He saw the night Dane had been brought into the trauma unit, his small body battered from the car accident.

He saw the white sheets on the gurney, soaked with his child's blood. Too much blood, way too much blood. And he'd known deep in his gut that Dane wouldn't make it to the operating room.

His only chance to live rested in Luke's hands.

Luke had saved so many who were considered past saving, working his life-giving magic in the emergency room. But that night his luck, all that magic, ran out. The skills he'd counted on, even taken for granted, had failed him.

Dane had been everything to him.

He'd been everything to Sylvie. Luke still saw the blame, the censure, in Sylvie's face, though she'd been too much of a lady to curse him aloud.

He'd seen the pain, though not blame, in his parents' eyes. They'd loved Dane, too.

And Luke had brought them all sheer anguish.

He needed to be on his way—to where, he didn't care. How long, he didn't know. He had too much pain, too much guilt, to wring from his soul.

Perhaps a lifetime of it.

Mariah had been hurt by what she saw as betrayal, and maybe it was betrayal. He only knew he'd caused her pain, pain she certainly didn't need.

Not now, not with Callie so ill.

She was a great mother. A good healer. She'd brought relief to his wounds—and even a little relief to his sorry soul. He knew everything she did for Callie was good medicine.

And everything she did, she did with love.

That ex-husband of hers was a fool to walk away from a woman like Mariah, a daughter as precious as Callie.

He hoped that someday Mariah would find a man worthy of her. A whole man. Not a man like Luke, who couldn't see his life beyond tomorrow.

That thought, however, brought a sharp stab of jealousy. Did he really want some other man tasting Mariah's sweetness, basking in her smile? In her beauty?

Damn his rotten hide, he didn't.

Luke cursed his soul—and decided he could use a walk, a long one. He needed to put some distance between himself and Mariah, needed to put some distance between himself and his failure—as a doctor, as a father, as a man.

The tears she'd been holding back began to fall. Mariah wasn't sure if they were for herself or for Callie. She wiped them away with the back of her hand.

She didn't have time for tears.

She had to tend to her daughter.

Mariah picked up the warm herbal packs she'd prepared and returned to her daughter's bedroom. Mariah was glad Luke had left.

She didn't need Callie upset by the emotional atmosphere between herself and Luke. And right now Mariah couldn't hold her feelings in check around the man.

"How're you doing now, sweetheart?" she asked.

Callie held her favorite doll, clutching it like a lifeline. "Same," she said. "You gonna hot pack me now?"

Unfortunately Callie knew the routine—they'd had to do this too many times in the past. And Mariah hated it for her child. "Why don't we read a couple of your books while the packs are on? Which ones would you like to hear?"

Callie named four, ones Mariah had read to her often, but they were still her favorites. Mariah placed the packs around Callie's tender joints, plumped her pillow then plucked the well-worn books from the shelf.

"Read this one first, Mommy," Callie instructed.

Mariah smiled, pulled up a chair and began to read.

The house was quiet except for the sound of her voice—and briefly she wondered if Luke had gone back to the cabin. She shouldn't care, shouldn't even allow thoughts of him to distract her.

Luke was a man with secrets, secrets he hadn't wanted to share. She'd seen the pain in his eyes, smoky shadows she didn't understand, shadows that surfaced likes ghosts in the mist.

Whatever had caused his pain, he intended to live with it.

It already lived with him.

By the time Mariah reached the end of the first story, Callie was looking more comfortable—and Mariah breathed a heavy sigh of relief.

This time the crisis would be short-lived.

And for Callie's sake, she was grateful.

Luke heard the familiar creak of the porch swing. It was Mariah, and from the uneven cadence of the swing, he knew she was restless, worried about Callie. The trip had been too hard for the little girl, and Luke felt badly about that.

Mariah was protective of her daughter, sometimes too much so, but Luke understood. She kept Callie wrapped in bunting to protect her from the disease that ate at her young joints.

Luke wished he could turn back life's cruel clock and protect *his* child. Keep him safe from everything he could—especially accidents like the horrific one that had taken his life.

The night was dark, the moon scudding behind the clouds as if afraid to show its face. He could barely make out Mariah's shape on the swing.

Was she still angry?

Luke knew that he had hurt her—though that had never been his intent. Perhaps he should have told her, explained who he was, why he was running.

He wished now that he had.

When he'd seen Callie in distress, his own training had kicked in and he'd gone to her, making his assessments of her condition as if she was a patient in the trauma unit.

And Mariah had noticed.

The woman was as perceptive as hell.

But he hadn't known how to talk about the awful heartbreak that had brought him so far from home. Home? Had he ever really had a home?

Certainly it wasn't that sterile condo on Lake Shore Drive, the one his cleaning lady spent more time in than he did.

He'd had a home with Sylvie once, when the three

of them had been a family. But even that home had seldom been graced with his presence.

His life had been the trauma center.

And in the end that life had cost him his son.

His walk tonight had solved nothing, hadn't eased his pain. Just brought him back here. To Mariah. He turned toward the porch and the sound of the swing, his thoughts on her. A short distance away he stopped. "How's Callie doing now?" he asked.

She didn't answer, but he saw her gaze settle on him, studying him as if he were bacteria under a microscope. He wanted to squirm under her intent perusal, but he held himself in check.

"She's better," she said finally, quietly.

Luke almost wished she'd rail at him, call him a slug or worse, but her study of his face went on as if she could divine what was in his evil heart. The night sounds began to get to him, the howl of a coyote in the distance, an answering call from closer.

"Why, Luke?" she asked him, her voice barely audible. "Why didn't you tell me you were a doctor? Why did you let me patch up your wounds when you could have done the job much better yourself? Or were you laughing at me? Laughing at my simple medicine?"

She stopped the motion of the porch swing with her foot, her bare foot—with sexy painted toenails. Her other foot was tucked up under her.

"You're wrong, Mariah. I wasn't laughing at you. All I could think about were your sweet hands on me. You made me hot, Mariah, *damned* hot."

That quieted her for a moment, as if she didn't know

what to say. Then the swing began to move again, slowly. She seemed to be mulling over his words.

"I've seen how Callie does. She thrives and it's because of you. And maybe, just maybe, *your* medicine can do more good than mine."

She turned her soulful gaze on him, as if deciding whether to believe him, studying him for signs of deceit or ridicule. Then she looked away, staring off into the dark night as if the answer might be there in the blackness.

"That still doesn't explain why, Luke—*why* you didn't tell me."

He'd hurt her—he owed her the truth. At least the part of it his soul could understand. He reached for the porch railing as if to anchor himself, so he didn't fly apart into a million pieces.

"I said I *was* a doctor, Mariah. Past tense. I gave up medicine. It wasn't a hard decision. I packed up what I needed to get by and left Chicago. I thought I could leave behind…the memories, as well. But that's something I haven't been able to do. The memories rode with me."

He could feel her gaze on him, though he couldn't bring himself to look up. "I had a son," he went on, a knot as big as the world lodged in his throat. "His name was Dane. And he died—died on his eighth birthday."

He heard her soft gasp. Knew that if he glanced at her, he'd see a stricken look on her face. And he wouldn't be able to go on. He hadn't talked about what had happened since that night, hadn't been able to do so with anyone.

"I-I'm sorry, Luke. You don't have to go on—not if it hurts to talk about it." Her words were soft, a whisper in the night. But he'd heard all the platitudes. At

Dane's funeral. All the polite things people say at a time like that.

He'd dismissed their well-intentioned words, convinced that none of them understood what he felt, how he felt, instead finding a certain relief that the accident had happened to someone else's child—not theirs.

It had been a source of Luke's anger, right along with the anger at himself that he hadn't been able to save his son, that he was a lousy doctor, a failure when it had counted most.

"I was the physician on duty that night in the trauma unit when they brought him in. He—he'd been…hit by a car."

Mariah swallowed hard. "Luke, I-I'm so sorry." She didn't know what more to say, how to comfort him. Or perhaps there was no comfort.

Not when a child died.

If it had been Callie—

She stopped that thought. The child had been Luke's, just as Callie was hers. And he'd suffered what no parent should ever have to suffer.

He stood there beside the porch. In the thin moonlight she could read the agony in his face. And now she knew what had put it there.

She stood up and went to him, though she wasn't certain her arms could be any comfort. She put them around him anyway and drew him close. He stiffened in her arms, but she wouldn't let him go. She held him, just held him, wishing with all her heart that she could ease the pain that gripped his soul.

"I'm sorry for your son," she whispered. "And I'm sorry for things I said."

He set her aside, drew her arms away from him. "It's okay. And it's late, Mariah. You need to go in to Callie. If…if you need anything in the night, if Callie gets worse…you know where I am," he said and turned to leave.

"Luke…"

He paused.

She couldn't let him go. Not this way. Not when he was hurting. Not when there were stormy shadows in his eyes where tears should have been.

She raised up and kissed him, a soft brush of her lips against his, but a kiss that came from her soul.

He raised his arms as if to put them around her, but hesitated. Mariah gave him another kiss, the temptation to make him linger so strong she could barely breathe.

"Mariah…" He whispered her name against her lips and his arms slid around her, drawing her tight against him.

She wished she knew how to banish his pain, wished things could be different for him. Then he kissed her, long, hard, passionately.

She felt him grow hard against her, proof he wanted her, and her heart pounded in her chest. What would it be like to make love with this man? At this moment she wanted to know, more than anything she'd ever wanted before.

His tongue sought the inside of her mouth and Mariah's lips parted, taking him in. His kiss was powerful, intense, and more. She'd never felt anything so overwhelming in her life.

Or so right.

The night closed around them—and Mariah wanted the kiss to go on forever.

But Luke stilled, and withdrew a fraction. "I want you, Mariah. I want you so much. But you should go in, to Callie."

"I know," she said, her voice with the same note of reluctance that she'd heard in his.

He planted a kiss on her neck, sending ripples of heat through her, despite the cooling night. "I meant what I said earlier. If you need me…"

She smiled. "I know."

Luke needed another walk, maybe something like a thirty-mile hike. Then he might be able to forget the taste of Mariah's comfort, the feel of her in his arms.

He'd told her about Dane–and something had shifted in his soul. He hadn't spoken of that night in the trauma unit since it had happened. There'd been no words to express the ache inside him, his failure, his loss.

He hadn't wanted sympathy. Hadn't wanted anyone's sympathy. Ever. It didn't make things easier for him, didn't lighten his overwhelming grief—or his regrets.

But Mariah's sweetness had eased something deep within him.

He sat down on the porch step. He didn't want to go back to the cabin, didn't want to face the four walls or listen to the coyotes howl at the moon.

The breeze stirred the porch swing, its slight creak making him wish Mariah was still here with him. He could still smell her fresh, feminine scent, as if the night breeze stirred it, too, and wafted it toward him.

He couldn't remember ever wanting a woman as much as he wanted her. But he couldn't make love to her, then ride out of her life forever.

Mariah had had one man do that to her already—Callie's father.

She deserved better.

She gave of herself to everyone, asking for nothing in return. Luke was sure there weren't many women around like that. At least, he hadn't crossed paths with any.

He was glad that Callie was better. And that, he was certain, was due to Mariah's herbs and her mother-love—something no doctor's medicine could give her.

Luke saw Mariah's bedroom light go out. Only then did he push off from the porch step and head back to the cabin, cursing himself every step of the way, for wanting to be in that room with her.

And in her bed.

Chapter Nine

Callie awoke the next morning feeling infinitely better, and Mariah gave a sigh of relief. She felt like she'd been waging a war against the grim disease for so long now, trying to keep Callie safe from its ravages.

And it was a war.

One she had to win.

She decided to spend today packaging up her herbs for mail order. Her living room looked like an assembly line of sorts, the plants she'd collected all hand-prepared, labeled with her new fancy labels and ready to be bagged for shipment.

Her business was a small operation, but it was already beginning to grow, which gave Mariah a bigger sense of security, a sense that she could support herself and her daughter.

This month she was including a catalog of the herbals

and their uses. The printing had been a big expense, but one she hoped would pay for itself in the end.

"Can I help, Mommy?" Callie asked.

She smiled over at her daughter, relieved that her eyes no longer glinted with fever and pain. It would take several more days for the inflammation to leave or at least subside to a more tolerable level. But Callie was better.

That was the important thing.

"You sure can, sweetheart. When I get each order ready, you can put one of these catalogs inside the package—okay?"

It was a small task, but Callie felt like she was lending a hand, and Mariah loved having her child close.

"Okay, Mommy."

An hour later they had the first batch ready to go out. Mariah had double-checked each one for accuracy and sealed the packages. She still had more orders to fill, plus the one large health-food store account she had in Phoenix. It was the one that brought in the most profit— and kept the wolf from their door.

She'd just reached for the next stack of order forms when Luke walked in, looking enticing enough to distract a nun. Try as she might not to react to his physicality, she did.

Every time.

"If you want breakfast, there's fresh-made cinnamon rolls in the kitchen and juice in the fridge," she told him.

"Not hungry—but I'll have some juice."

"Can I have juice with Luke?" Callie asked.

Mariah was losing her workforce.

"You may," she said, and Callie bounded across the room toward Luke.

His medical radar was on alert, Mariah noticed, as he studied Callie's gait, her liveliness, her sparkle—all things that would reflect on her condition.

She wondered if he realized that down deep he was still a doctor—and always would be. He may have turned his back on medicine, but it was still very much a part of him.

"You're looking perkier today, princess," he said, tugging on her long beribboned braid.

"Mmm-hmm. Mommy helped me—and now I'm all better."

"I can see that." He turned and gave Mariah a smile. "You're a good healer, Mariah."

Her heart did a somersault at the compliment. Coming from Luke the words meant a lot. She was sorry she'd doubted him last night, believed that he'd tricked her somehow by not revealing his past.

He'd had reasons for his reticence, and she hoped that by talking about it last night, some of his pain had abated. At least this morning the shadows seemed to be absent from his eyes.

"Thanks," she said. "Callie's *much* better. But I'm not sure the herbs are the total reason. Callie's a strong little girl."

Mariah was continually amazed at how quickly a child could heal. And frightened by how quickly one could go sour.

"Speaking of herbs," he said, "what's all this?"

"*This* is how I pay the bills. I have a mail-order business, selling to a small list of customers."

His mouth quirked up in a half smile, a mouth Mariah knew the taste of—intimately. A shiver ran up her spine at the memory of it on hers.

"Looks to me like you have enough herbs here to fill a major warehouse."

"A small but *growing* list," she corrected. "You and Callie go have your juice, then I plan to put you both to work."

"It's fun," Callie said. "Mommy lets me help."

"Is the pay good?" he asked Callie, which made her giggle.

"No pay," Mariah answered for her daughter. "But the work is rewarding."

"I hate jobs like that. No pay, all reward."

"No complaining," she said, then watched as the pair disappeared into the kitchen.

A short while later they were back. "Mmm, those cinnamon rolls were delicious," he said.

She turned and gave him a look. "I thought you said you weren't hungry."

He patted his flat stomach. "I couldn't resist."

Mariah knew all about being unable to resist. It was a malady she had whenever the man was anywhere close to her. She pushed the thought from her mind. She had orders to fill—and that meant no fantasizing about Luke Phillips.

"Are you ready to work?" she asked him.

"What do you want me to do? I don't know a thing about herbs or mail order."

"Then it's time you learn."

She gave him a quick rundown of her little business and how it worked. He listened, absorbing her explanation, occasionally asking a question or offering a smile.

His smiles were hard to deal with. She wondered if he knew that, knew the effect he had on women.

"I'm impressed," he said when she had finished.

That pleased her more than she wanted to let on.

"I'm not paying you to be impressed," she said, pretending indifference. "I'm paying you to work."

"Babe, you're not paying me at all."

She gave a small, choked laugh. She liked it when he called her *babe*. It wasn't used derisively but as…an *intimacy*. "Do you want this job or not?"

He pretended to consider it.

"Get busy," she ordered.

Luke did, placing the packets of herbs in the appropriate mailers and checking them off the order sheet. Simple enough, Luke thought, as long as he kept his attention on what he was doing—and off his pretty boss.

"Does this mail-order operation bring in a good income?" he asked, seriously curious about this small business of hers.

Mariah was a capable woman. He admired her ingenuity and that she was able to manage without a full-time job.

A job would be difficult, considering Callie's illness. And, knowing Mariah, she would want to look after her daughter herself, rather than entrusting her to a sitter.

She looked up from her work for a moment, and Luke saw the deep intelligence in her green eyes. Intelligence was always a big turn-on for him—but then, with Mariah, *everything* turned him on.

"It doesn't make us wealthy," she said, "but it provides for what we need."

But not the extras, Luke suspected. No trips to Disneyland for Callie, not even a computer to help Mariah's business run smoother—depending, no doubt, on less modern means to promote her products. "You deserve more, Mariah."

She deserved the world.

She gave a soft smile. "Growing up Hopi taught me there are more important things than material riches— but at times…at times I do wish there was more."

Her glance toward her daughter told him she meant more for Callie, not for herself. Mariah would do without to be certain Callie had whatever she might need.

"So, how often do you do this—mail out orders, I mean?"

"Each month."

"And how often do you gather herbs?"

She gave another smile. "Every chance I get. That's the part I enjoy the most. I love being out among the rocks and mesas, wandering the cool valleys. The hardest part is the preparation—the drying, the grinding, extracting the oils, and of course, all the packaging and labeling."

"I admire your knowledge," he said. "And your determination to help relieve other people's pain."

She glanced up and held his gaze for a long moment. "It's not so different from what you do, Luke."

"What I *used* to do," he corrected.

She saw the shadows in his eyes shift and darken. She'd overstepped her bounds. She shouldn't have said that. She had no right.

Luke was living with a pain she could only imagine. Mariah had her daughter; Luke had *lost* his son. He had no one. "I'm sorry," she said.

"No need to apologize. It—it's just a fact."

An unfortunate fact, Mariah thought sadly. Luke had so much to offer, so much to give—but he no longer believed it. She wished…wished there was something she could do, some way to make him believe again, some way to convince him that sometimes you fail, despite everything you do.

Luke added the last of the items into the mailer and checked them off the list. "Done," he said.

"Completely done," Mariah added. "That's the last of the orders." She took the one he'd just finished and held it out to Callie for the catalog contribution, then sealed up the package. "I'll take them to the post office later."

"How about we take them to the post office this afternoon, then stop in at Rudy's for an early dinner?" Luke suggested.

"Pizza!" Callie said.

Mariah smiled. Of course it was pizza—it was the only thing Rudy's served. She glanced at Callie, then at Luke—and saw two expectant faces.

She knew when she was beaten.

"Okay," she said. "Rudy's it is."

Rudy's was already filling with patrons by the time they'd dropped off Mariah's packages at the post office and strolled over to the small restaurant.

Many of the same group who'd greeted Luke with stares of curiosity the last time he was here now greeted him with smiles and waves. As if he were their new best friend.

He returned the smiles and greetings, feeling like someone had made him a resident of the town when he wasn't looking.

And that bothered him.

He no longer belonged in Chicago, with all its painful memories, but neither did he belong here in Sunrise.

"Looks like you've made a few friends, Luke Phillips," Mariah said as she followed him toward the back of the place.

"Yeah—maybe I'll run for mayor," he said with a hint of sarcasm to his voice.

"I want to sit here," Callie said, pulling out a chair from a table, thankfully distant from the group.

Luke helped her onto her chair, then held one out for Mariah.

Luke didn't want to make friends with the townsfolk. Nor was he going to be here long enough to fall in love with the woman sitting beside him, he reminded himself.

Just in case he might foolishly be considering it.

They ordered a sausage and pepperoni pizza with extra cheese, and when it finally arrived, Mariah took a large slice. "I'm starved after all that work today," she said.

Luke took a slice, but he wasn't as hungry as he thought. Reminders choked him, reminders that he had more miles to cover, more distance to put between himself and his past. He'd never thought of himself as a coward, but maybe that's just what he was. But how did a man stand and fight demons he couldn't see?

He'd set out on this strange odyssey because he couldn't bear to stay at the hospital. Not when every accident victim brought in reminded him of Dane and that awful night.

For six shifts a week for nearly four months he fought down the terror that rose up like so much bile in his throat. Sweat broke out on his forehead and his once-agile fingers had lost their surety, shaking like an aspen leaf in a windstorm. A doctor couldn't work with shaky hands—or an even shakier belief in himself.

Callie kept up a lively banter during dinner, talking a blue streak—and Luke was glad. It gave him time to curse his sorry life.

"Why so quiet?" Mariah asked him a short time later.

The woman didn't miss a thing, Luke thought.

"Sorry—guess I'm not very good company tonight." He added a smile, but he doubted it would fool her.

It hadn't even succeeded in fooling him.

Her gaze remained on his face, roving over it, searching it. Luke picked up the conversation and tried to keep up his end. He didn't want Mariah worrying about him.

She had enough of that without including Luke and his problems.

Mariah thought about Luke's silence all the way home.

By the time she had Callie tucked into bed for the night, her concern hadn't lessened. She knew the weight he carried on those broad shoulders of his. Everyone had a breaking point.

Even Luke.

Would the breaking point come before he found his own forgiveness?

Quietly she closed Callie's bedroom door—and went in search of him. She found him out back, quietly studying the sky.

"Want some company?" she asked.

She saw a flash of warmth in his blue eyes before the darkness took hold again. "I was about to take a walk by the stream. Want to join me?"

She gave a slow nod, wondering if she trusted herself alone with him in the moonlight.

He set the pace, slow and rambling. The moon was vivid tonight, the stars bright. A slight breeze rustled through the cottonwood trees.

"Something's on your mind," she said. "I'm a good listener."

He didn't answer for a few more yards. "I'm fine," he said. "I'm just…restless."

"Restless."

"Yeah—I need to be getting on my way again."

Neither of them spoke, the silence stretching between them like an oversize elephant in an elevator no one wanted to admit to seeing.

Finally Mariah broke the silence. "Do you have someplace you intend to go?"

He averted his gaze and didn't answer—and Mariah's soul ached for him. Luke wouldn't find peace by riding to nowhere. But he didn't seem to realize that.

"I wish there was an herb for a broken heart," she said. "I'd give it to you."

They'd reached the stream. It burbled over the rocks, a quiet murmur in the background. He took her hand and kissed her fingers, then her open palm. "You could make a man want to stick around," he said, his voice low, strangled.

Mariah drew in a sigh. "That's not true," she said. "Will didn't have any burning desire to stay."

"He was a fool." His lips brushed her eyelids, the tip of her nose, then her softly parted mouth.

Mariah felt a slow heat melt through her. Never had

a kiss affected her like this. What was it about Luke, this stranger, that made her lose her usual good judgment?

He was a man chased by his pain, a pain she wished she could wrest from him—but she could no more heal him than she was able to heal Callie.

If wishing could do it, if love—

Mariah tried to escape that thought. She couldn't fall in love with Luke. He came from another world, a world she didn't know, would never know.

One day, when he finally healed, he'd return to Chicago and his medicine. And Mariah knew that that was where he belonged.

She knew—but at the moment Luke's heated mouth on hers dissolved every rational thought in her head.

Just one more moment, one more taste of this man, one more second of this wonder, she promised, then she would pull away and reclaim her sanity.

Mariah was killing him with her passion, her softness—and Luke knew he'd only have himself to blame when the kiss ended and he was plain miserable without her in his bed.

She fit against him so perfectly, felt so right in his arms. His tongue teased at her lips until she opened for him. Oh, damn! Was he in heaven or hell?

She tasted so sweet, now sultry, then sweet again— how could a woman be both? He didn't know, but Mariah was—and he wanted her so damned bad.

Her feminine scent played havoc with his thoughts, fogged his senses, set him on fire. He couldn't remember a woman ever making him feel this way.

Her hands ran over his chest, then up to his neck, her

fingers clasping at the back and drawing his mouth down harder on hers. He was in agony.

He slid his hands up her sides, under her blouse, and found her breasts. They filled his palms, her nipples hard and aware. He pictured her naked and ready, wanting him.

Ignore the fantasy, his brain warned him. He didn't need his body growing any harder than it was. But try as he might, he couldn't banish the thought.

She leaned into him, pressing against his hardness. He gave a low, guttural groan. "Mariah, do you know what you're doing to me?"

"Mmm—I think so."

He was lost.

He kissed her sultry mouth, tasted her want that matched his own. His hands slipped her blouse off in one smooth motion, then her bra, exposing her silky breasts to the moonlight, the starlight—and his own eyes. She was beautiful, wondrous—and he grew harder still.

He wanted to scoop her up in his arms and take her to his bed, but Mariah was so much a woman of the earth, this magical landscape, he wanted to make love to her here, the earth beneath them, the night sky above.

Her hands went to his waist and tugged his shirt from his jeans, working it slowly up his chest, her hands touching his bare skin as they went.

And Luke was sure he'd never felt anything so erotic in his life.

Mariah sucked in a breath. She'd seen this man without his shirt before, but this moment, in the moonlight, wanting him as she did, he looked even more devastating. Her hands strayed and touched, reveling in the crisp sprinkling of chest hair, his taut male nipples.

She heard his sharp inhalation of breath and knew her touch excited him.

In a fraction of a second he had her shorts and panties off and she was lying flat on her back in the soft, thick grass. It felt incredibly cool against her overheated skin. And then he was standing over her, jeans shucked and body naked.

An image that would forever be seared into her brain.

His body looked bronzed in the moonlight, bronzed, beautiful—and ready.

"Make love to me, Luke…." Her voice sounded strange, husky, not really her own.

"You're sure?" he asked, his voice sounding as different as hers.

She gave him a smile. "Very sure."

He lowered himself to her and fit her body beneath him. His mouth found hers in a hot, hungry kiss. Her arms wound around his neck, and his hands went roaming over her in a caress that took her breath away. His fingers were masterful, knowing every waiting inch of her body.

He kissed her neck, nipped her earlobes, then trailed a chain of kisses between her breasts down to the flatness of her stomach. He was setting her on fire.

He touched her heated core, making sure she could take him, that she was ready. She pulsed against his touch and arched toward him, wanting him, wanting him now. Suddenly, he pulled back from her.

"Protection," he said and grabbed his jeans, digging in his pockets until he came up with a small foil packet.

Mariah hadn't thought of it, either, but then she hadn't had many blazing affairs. Only the one she'd had with Will when they were too young and foolish to realize life happened, and that this wasn't a game for adolescents.

"Damn thing," Luke cursed, all thumbs, working the package.

Maybe he wasn't a man who did this every night. If fumbling with a condom was any proof, he didn't. She reached over and took the packet, undid it, then slipped it on him.

He sucked in a breath. "Easy with those hands, sweetheart."

Mariah smiled at the power she had, a power she lost in the very next moment when he took over. He kissed his way down her body, lower, then lower still, his mouth finding her feminine heat. She writhed beneath the onslaught, the ecstasy driving her wild with need.

When she could barely stand it a second more, he drew back and slipped deep into her. He paused, letting her adjust to him. Then he began to move, slowly at first, then with a rhythm that stole her sanity, heat building until there was no thought, only sensations, wondrous sensations. She arched against him, wanting more, wanting this to never end.

Finally she exploded, fireworks going off as she felt herself shatter around him. Another thrust and Luke followed her over the edge.

They lay still, sated, Luke's arm resting across her possessively. No regrets, Mariah told herself. She'd gone into this with her eyes wide-open. She knew this man, knew his destiny lay somewhere beyond here, far from Sunrise, far from her and Callie.

"You're awfully quiet," he said, rising up on one elbow to look at her. His arm stayed where it was, holding her lightly.

"Just coming down to earth," she said.

He smiled, and his eyes in the moonlight carried no dark shadows. She snuggled into him, absorbing his body heat. Then his hand began to move, gently, slowly, bringing her skin to life.

"You're beautiful, Mariah."

She smiled, all too aware of what he was doing to her body, igniting little fires beneath his fingertips.

He kissed her lips. "I'm going to make love to you slowly," he whispered, and she knew he meant every word as his fingers caressed and stroked, bringing sensations alive all over again.

Memories to store away after he's gone? *Don't go there,* Mariah ordered herself.

No regrets.

His lips followed where his fingers had been, kissing her breasts each one in turn, his tongue lazily circling her nipples as if he had forever to sample her. She felt the heat build deep within her and she wrapped her arms around his neck.

He took her hands and drew them away. "Don't interrupt," he said.

Every path he'd taken earlier, he took slowly now. His fingers probed her femininity, stroking, teasing,

She was losing her mind under his assault. She wanted him, wanted him inside her. But he was determined to torture her until she couldn't take any more.

"Luke…" she called his name on a near-scream and her body arched as sensations too exquisite to bear rocked her.

Only then did he slide between her thighs and enter her, plunging deeper, intensity building until they both came apart in each other's arms.

Chapter Ten

No regrets! Mariah said to herself as she pulled another weed from her garden. *No regrets, no regrets, no regrets.* Oh, no! She'd pulled up a fledgling coriander, its soft, soily roots dangling.

Her garden had always been therapy for her, but she wasn't sure it could do much for her mental state today. She dug a small hole and tucked the plant back into the loamy earth, brushed dirt from its leaves and hoped it would survive the unwarranted shock she'd just put it through.

Frustrated tears stung her eyes, but she blinked them away. What was wrong with her today? But Mariah knew what was wrong—she'd fallen in love with Luke Phillips.

Fool, fool, fool.

Three more weeds bit the dust. At least she hoped they were weeds. She glanced at the results of her fury.

Yes, weeds—thankfully.

Luke's bike sat a few yards away. Soon it would be operational again, and he would ride away—out of her life.

Fool, fool, fool—more weeds were gone.

And so was her heart.

Hopelessly.

What would she do when he left? How would she pick up the pieces of her life and go on?

Mariah didn't have the answer.

Just then she caught sight of Una coming across the yard. She jerked off her gardening gloves and stood up. It was time to quit before the woman noticed her lunacy.

"Father Sky! It looks like you don't have good sense bein' out here in this heat," Una scolded.

In truth, Mariah hadn't noticed the heat.

She forced a smile. "I was just going indoors to check on Callie. Would you like to come in and have some blueberry cobbler? I made it this morning."

When she couldn't sleep because she'd been thinking of Luke—and what had happened between them last night.

Fool!

"Blueberry cobbler? I'm right behind you," Una said.

Mariah hoped this wasn't an invitation to trouble. The old woman's radar was unusually sharp—and Mariah didn't need her picking up on her overwrought emotions.

Not today.

Not after last night.

"Where is this young man of yours?" Una asked as they reached the kitchen.

Mariah went to the sink to wash the gardening dirt

from her hands. "Luke isn't my young man—he isn't my *anything*," she said.

She knew Una worried about her, but she didn't need to. Mariah was fine. She'd *be* fine.

Luke would leave—and she would recover.

Una didn't look convinced—and Mariah was afraid her feelings about Luke were hanging out there for everyone to see.

"I'll go get Callie," she said. "Will you cut the cobbler and pour the iced tea?"

Una agreed, and Mariah was relieved to escape the room. Her neighbor could be meddling. She probably thought Luke was the perfect man for her.

But Mariah knew he wasn't.

Callie wasn't playing with her dolls in the living room where Mariah had left her. Her dolls and doll clothes lay there abandoned. Then she heard Callie's little-girl chatter coming from the front porch. She started for the door.

"Callie—"

Mariah stopped when she saw who her daughter was talking to.

Luke.

"So why are you fixing the swing?" Callie asked, her pert face upturned to his as she watched him work.

"Because it has a noisy squeak, bright eyes."

He looked so handsome, his face tanned, his eyes as blue as the sky. His navy-blue polo shirt hugged his broad shoulders. Mariah knew every muscle of those shoulders, every inch of that hard body—and a hot blush crept to her cheeks.

Just then Luke noticed her at the door. Her heart stammered at his heated glance.

Callie glanced up, too. "Hi, Mommy. I'm watching Luke fix our swing."

"So I see." She didn't realize how sexy a man could look, holding an oil can. But Luke did. "I came to see if you wanted some blueberry cobbler," she said to Callie.

"Luke...?" She added him to the invitation, though she wasn't sure her emotions were ready for him just yet.

"Cobbler—*yeah!*" Callie said, and clambered up from the porch step where she'd been sitting.

"Una's in the kitchen," she told her. "She'll pour you a glass of milk."

Callie headed inside and Mariah was alone with Luke. His gaze slid lazily over her and Mariah's breath caught in her throat. Why did she always react like this to him?

"You look beautiful today," he said.

She smiled at the compliment. "Do you want to come in for cobbler?"

"Save me a piece. I'll be in as soon as I'm done here."

"Luke, you don't have to fix—"

"I know I don't have to," he interrupted.

Luke had been going crazy, thinking about last night, remembering the feel of Mariah in his arms, the taste of her, how she felt beneath him. He *had* to keep busy.

She gave him a smile and his heart kicked at his ribs. Suddenly Luke wasn't sure there were enough jobs in the world to keep his mind off this woman.

"Don't forget the cobbler," she said. "And, Luke—"

"Yes?"

"Thank you." Her voice was a soft, sultry whisper.

Oh, yes—he had to keep busy.

He stared at the doorway long after she'd gone back

inside, the oil can in his hand half-forgotten. The porch swing. The task of oiling the other hinge would take him all of thirty seconds. Then what would he do to keep his mind off this woman who fueled his fantasies?

He gave the remaining hinge a squirt of oil, wiped off the excess with the rag and checked his handiwork with a test push. Barely a sound.

Now all he had to do was find something to occupy his thoughts until he could make the repairs to his cycle—and ride out.

Leaving here, leaving Mariah, would take all the strength he had. He'd never be able to forget making love to her. Or forget that he *shouldn't* have.

But he couldn't undo what had happened last night.

All he could do was not make the situation any worse by letting it happen again.

That night Mariah sat on the front porch leisurely rocking the swing that Luke had fixed earlier today. It was pleasant not having the squeak to interrupt her reverie. She'd never noticed the noise before or how irritating it was.

Had she properly thanked him for fixing it? She couldn't remember. Her thoughts had been scattered ever since…

Since making love with him.

Luke was enough man to make a woman forget her own name with just a look. Making love with him increased her brainlessness to near-comatose.

After getting Callie to sleep, she'd been tempted to slip out the back door to the cabin, wanting Luke to hold her, kiss her, *make love to her* one more time.

But that would only make things more difficult—and invite more heartache than was already coming.

There was nothing in Sunrise to keep a man here, much less a man like Luke, a man used to big-city life, big-city hospitals—and women who didn't sit on a front porch swing dreaming foolishly under the stars.

She'd been content with her life before Luke had come riding into it. No, she thought—that wasn't wholly true.

Something had been missing.

And when Luke had held her in his arms, she knew what that something was.

A man to love and who loved her.

A man to share her pain and her joy.

A man to grow old with.

A single tear rolled down her cheek and dripped onto her leg, bare below her denim shorts. She felt its heat sear her skin.

There was no future for her with Luke. She'd known that from the beginning—but her crazy heart hadn't listened to her brain. Hadn't she promised herself she'd never let another man hurt her?

Will had done it cruelly, selfishly.

But with Luke, Mariah could only blame herself.

With Will she'd been young, an innocent. But she was no longer foolishly young. She was a woman, a woman with responsibilities she'd thought came first, *should* have come first.

Instead she'd walked into this relationship with Luke with eyes wide-open. He'd never once said he loved her, never said he wanted a life with her—but her heart hadn't wanted to listen.

She'd worked to heal his wounds.

Had her heart believed it could heal the wounds of his soul, as well?

On Tuesday Luke was awake early, ready for the drive to Cottonwood to pick up his cycle part.

Una had agreed to watch Callie, so Mariah could go with him. She and Una both needed things from the grocery store in Cottonwood—and Mariah would pick up the items.

Having her along for the day pleased him as well as set him on edge. He hadn't forgotten his vow to keep hands-off—and he intended to stick to it.

Yesterday he'd busied himself cleaning out the shed behind her house. He didn't know how she found anything in it. The meager tools she had were as old as the hills, but she hadn't wanted to part with a single one.

Here in Sunrise, she'd explained, no one threw anything out. They didn't have stores on every corner like larger towns, and she never knew when she, or a neighbor, might need one of those tools.

So Luke had found some old rusty nails in a sack in the shed, along with an equally rusty hammer, and spent the next few hours pounding nails into one wall as makeshift hooks to suspend the tools from. Then he tackled the rest of the mess, even chasing a furry critter or two from the cool interior.

At the end of the day he had the old shed organized, and was sufficiently tired enough to eat a bowl of Mariah's green chile stew, then tumble into bed, too weary to even dream about her.

But today, with Mariah along, the battle would be uphill all the way.

He swallowed hard as she climbed into the cab of the truck. Her soft-flowered scent teased at his senses, and he knew he was in trouble already.

"Sorry, I'm late," she said, squirming into the passenger seat. "I had a few last-minute instructions for Una."

"No problem," he said and eased the old truck down the driveway to the road. "Was Callie disappointed she couldn't go along?"

"She was—but I explained that I didn't want her to have a flare-up of her disease. And she understood. She didn't like it, but she understood."

"Maybe we can bring her back a treat."

She gave him a frown. "I thought I was the one who spoiled her. You, Luke Phillips, do a good job of it, as well."

"Yeah, well, she's a darling kid."

Like her mother, Luke thought. Mariah's dark hair was plaited in a long braid that hung down her back, her skin dewy-fresh, a touch of color to her lips, the only makeup she wore.

And Luke was well tempted to taste that mouth this morning, test its passion, but he'd promised himself he wouldn't do that. It wouldn't stop with a single kiss— and he knew that.

They made the trip to Cottonwood in less time than they had the other day. Without Callie along, Luke could take the horrible roads at a faster clip. Still he avoided the worst of the dips and ruts, knowing Mariah would like to keep her old truck in one piece.

He stopped at the cycle shop first, ready to take the clerk's head off if the part wasn't in—but Luke hadn't needed to worry. It had arrived with the early morning delivery.

Luke would have his transportation back at long last.

In addition to the cycle part, he bought a few tools he and Eli might need to install it, paid for his purchases, thanked the clerk and headed for the door.

"Want to have lunch somewhere?" he asked as he returned to the truck.

Mariah was beautiful, he thought as she looked up. He loved her green eyes, the long, slender column of her neck, her pretty mouth. Her deep-blue top had a scoop neck, but Luke tried to steer his gaze upward, where it was somewhat safer.

"There's an outdoor café here, if you'd like to try it. The food is good."

He started up the truck. "Sounds fine to me."

A short while later they were seated at a table under a large shade tree. A soft breeze fluttered the leaves, making the spot enchanting and cool.

Romantic.

But that was a thought Mariah needed to get out of her head. Luke now had the cycle part he needed—and he'd be leaving.

Tomorrow?

The next day?

Whichever it was, Sunrise, Arizona, would soon be nothing more than a memory to him. Oh, he might remember her on some soft, quiet night, but that would be the extent of it.

She would never forget him, though. Never forget the taste of him, the feel of his hard body against hers as they made love that night in the moonlight.

She'd already begun memorizing his face, the shape of his ear, his mouth when he smiled, the dark shadows in his eyes when he was unable to hide them.

No, she'd never be able to forget this tall, rugged man who could take her breath away, this man her heart had fallen in love with.

"You look like you're miles away. What are you thinking?"

She'd been caught daydreaming, something she never used to do. Until Luke. She used to be a sane and sensible woman, but somewhere along the way, she'd turned into a foolish one.

And she didn't want Luke knowing that.

She tried a smile, hoping to keep it steady on her lips. "I was just thinking that it's a good day for you. Your part came in, and when we get back, you can install it, then—" Her voice cracked, something she'd hoped to avoid. "Then…you can be on your way."

She unwrapped her cloth napkin, not wanting him to see the pain in her eyes, the tears forming there.

"Mariah…"

She smoothed the napkin carefully over her lap. "What?"

"Mariah, look at me."

She struggled to blink away the moisture in her eyes, then gave him a brief glance.

"I—I don't like going, Mariah, but I have to. My life came apart the night I lost Dane. I tried for months to hold it together but I couldn't. I'm no longer a whole person. Maybe I never will be. I have to find that out. I have to find out if I can live with this self-hatred that rules my soul. And maybe I can find that out somewhere along the way."

"And if you don't? Do you keep running?"

It took a long moment but he finally answered. "Yes."

Her voice was a whisper. "You need to go back, Luke, back where you belong, back to the healing you do there."

"Past tense," he said harshly. "Healing I *used* to do. I lost it, lost the ability to save anyone, Mariah. Even myself."

Just then the waitress appeared with their lunch and the conversation drew to a halt.

But Mariah knew the shadows were there in his eyes again. He wouldn't go back to Chicago, but would instead ride off to battle his demons alone. A knot formed in her throat. Luke was a man who had so much to give, but he no longer believed it.

"Don't worry about me, Mariah."

He reached across the table for her hand. Their fingers linked and held for a long moment. Mariah wondered how such a gesture could seem so intimate. Then he drew his hand from hers and she felt the loss of his heat, the intimacy.

"I will worry," she said. "Don't ask me not to, Luke."

She took a bite of the fancy little croissant sandwich the waitress had brought her, but it suddenly tasted like sawdust in her throat. The romantic little spot in the café's tree-shaded courtyard no longer seemed so idyllic.

A chill ran through her body.

She wanted to reach for his fingers again, lace hers through his—but the goodbye had begun. It was time to draw away, the instinctive human attempt to avoid the pain that was sure to come.

* * *

Luke trailed behind Mariah with the shopping cart as she scanned the grocery aisle shelves, studied labels—and the price.

The few times he had bothered to go to the supermarket, he hadn't given a hang about price or quantity, just tossed what he wanted into the basket and moved on to the next item.

As a doctor he'd, of course, considered heart-smart foods and only occasionally indulged in chips, dips and ice cream. But Mariah had to be certain she was getting quality nutrition for the small amount of money she had to spend.

He had to admire her, making it through life with her daughter the best way she could, never asking for a thing, only giving—giving to all those around her.

Including his sorry soul.

Luke had tucked money into the cookie jar where she kept her reserve of cash and grocery coupons. He'd eaten more than his share of food while he was there.

If he'd handed the cash to her she'd have complained, told him he was a guest and wouldn't take the money. He only hoped he'd be gone before she noticed how much was in her stash.

"Hey, look at this. Callie would love to have one of these," Luke said, drawing Mariah's attention to a colorful kite he'd spotted at the front of the store.

It was bright orange, green and purple with a myriad of flowers dancing across the kite's fabric. This was no cheapie, either. It was sturdily made with a long string to feed out as the kite soared.

He'd bought one for Dane for his fifth birthday—but

he couldn't remember if he'd taken him out to fly it. He swallowed the lump in his throat, knowing he'd never have the chance now.

But he could show Callie how to fly it.

"Luke, you'll spoil her."

But he marched up to the checker and paid for the item.

Mariah was annoyed with him. Callie would *love* the kite, of course, but what would happen when Luke was gone, out of their lives forever?

Callie thought the world of the man—and Luke bringing her gifts would only make it harder when he left.

She pushed the cart toward the checkout lane, hoping she had everything on Una's list and her own. She pulled out her coupons to hand the clerk, then carefully counted out her money.

There was more cash than she should have. Had Una handed her too much? She counted it again with the same results. Before she could figure it out the clerk was asking for her coupons. Mariah handed them over and tried to keep her mind focused on what she was doing.

When the final bill was rung up, the coupons deducted, the money handed to the clerk, Mariah had lots of cash left.

Luke.

Had he slipped the money into her cookie jar? She shot him a glance, but he was handily hefting the sacks into the cart, along with the kite he'd bought for Callie.

Mariah followed behind him as he pushed the grocery basket toward the truck and loaded the sacks into the back. She waved the leftover money at him. "I seem to have a small windfall left after I paid the clerk. You wouldn't happen to know how that happened, would you?"

He gave her a choirboy look. "Maybe you don't know how to count."

"I can count as well as a tax collector," she said, but he ushered her into the truck and tucked the sack holding Callie's kite in beside her.

"Be careful with the kite," he said. "I don't want it smashed before Callie and I can fly it."

Chapter Eleven

Luke carried the groceries in and set them on the kitchen counter. Callie bounded into the room with a big kiss for her mother and a wide smile for Luke.

He wanted to tell her about the surprise he'd brought back for her, but it could wait. Besides, there wasn't enough wind to launch a kite right now.

"Thank you for picking up my things," Una said. "Do I owe you any extra?"

Mariah shot Luke a chastising glower, then turned back to her neighbor. "No—it seems I had plenty."

She was still miffed about the money. Luke quickly changed the subject. "Is Eli around? I have the part for the cycle," he told Una. "I'm ready to get to work anytime."

"He's around—over at the house. Moping, I'm afraid."

Luke raised an eyebrow. "What's wrong?"

"It's his father," she said. "Jimmy's been at the

bottle again. Eli hates that. And he knows how it worries me."

Luke frowned. "Is Jimmy home?"

Una gave a bleak look. "No, he took off in that old rattletrap truck of his. I hide his keys, but he always manages to find them. I'm afraid one of these days he's gonna kill himself—or somebody else."

Luke saw the anxiety lining Una's face. "C'mon," he told her. "I'll carry your groceries home for you—and maybe I can have a talk with Eli."

The words were out before Luke realized it. There wasn't a thing he could do to remedy the awful situation this family was in. He was a doctor, not a magician. Besides, he'd given up saving people.

He wasn't very good at it these days.

"Anything you can do would help Eli. He thinks the sun rises and sets in you—and that motor-sickle you got."

He smiled at the old woman's word for his bike—and hefted her two grocery bags from the counter. If he knew Eli, he was quick to correct his grandmother's pronunciation. And if he knew Una, she planned to go right on calling the bike a motor-sickle.

He started toward the back door after her, carrying the groceries, but Mariah put a restraining hand on his arm. "Thank you, Luke," she said.

"For what?"

"For saying you'd talk to Eli."

Luke hadn't said he *would*. He'd said *maybe*—but Mariah was smiling up at him like he could pull a rabbit out of a hat. Damn—all he wanted to do was get to work on his bike.

"I only said I'd have a word with the kid. Don't go expecting anything more than that, Mariah."

But Mariah's smile didn't waver.

And Luke had the feeling he'd just bought into a new problem.

Mariah had Callie down for a little quiet time. Now it was her turn, she thought as she put on the kettle for a cup of herbal tea. While she waited for the water to boil she peered out the window.

Luke was out back, working on his cycle.

Eli was with him, handling his share of the work.

She was thankful that Luke had offered to speak with the boy about his father's drinking. If Eli could open up to Luke about his feelings…

Mariah didn't know exactly what she thought Luke might be able to do—she just knew Eli could use a friend.

She gave a small sigh and moved away from the window. She could use a friend, as well—a friend to talk to, to share things with, a friend who stuck extra money in her cookie jar for groceries when he didn't have to, who bought bright-colored kites for her daughter just to please her. A friend who cared enough to talk to a young neighbor boy about his father.

She felt tears gather in her eyes and tried to blink them away. Luke would leave such a big hole in her heart when he left. When would it be? Today? Tomorrow? Mariah didn't want to think about it.

But she knew that wouldn't change the certainty.

When her tea had steeped she sat down at the kitchen table with her cup and wrapped her hands around its warmth. It was her own special blend, created from her healing herbs—a few to calm and soothe, a few for aroma and body.

She intended to add it to the mail-order catalog next month, hoping it would sell well.

But Mariah knew it would take a lot more than a cup of herbal tea to quiet her mood today. Luke had the replacement part he needed, and once he'd made the repairs to his cycle, there would be no reason for him to stay.

Mariah had known that from the beginning, had warned herself not to get too close, to let herself care.

Or…fall in love.

She and Luke came from separate worlds. Hers was here with Callie, close to the special herbs that could help her. His was back in Chicago, or some other big city. In his E.R. where he could do so much good.

Just then she heard the roar of the bike's engine, someone romping on the gas in noisy fits and starts. A moment later the big, silver beast hurtled down the driveway and out onto the road.

She listened—listened until there was silence again.

And knew that soon that silence would become permanent.

She carried her cup to the sink and emptied its contents down the drain. She didn't want the tea.

She wanted Luke.

"So what do you think?" Luke asked over the roaring sound of the Harley.

They took the corner out of Mariah's driveway and onto the road.

"It's way cool," Eli yelled back.

He was seated behind Luke, hanging on to him for dear life. Would Luke have done this with his son one day? Gone careening around corners? Outrunning the wind? Would Dane have howled with excitement the way Eli was doing?

That was something Luke would never know.

He tamped down his pain—and his anger at himself. He should have been able to save Dane that night. If only he'd been smarter, more skilled, more—

But he couldn't go back to that night, couldn't undo what had already happened—however much he wanted to.

This place, these few days with Mariah, had given him a temporary respite from life, from reminders of that horrific night. But his cycle was up and running now. It was time for him to leave. Time to take his miserable soul on down the highway.

After enough miles maybe he…

Luke didn't think there were enough miles, enough highways, to make him forget.

He raced over the hills and around the curves. The bike handled easily. His leg no longer hurt. His shoulder had healed.

Mariah had worked her magic.

Now he had to find some way to forget the feel of those hands, her hot, branding kisses, the way she made love to him—so open and free.

But Luke knew there weren't enough miles or highways for that, either.

Finally he turned the bike around and headed back. "That's enough of a test run for now," he told Eli.

"Okay, sure."

There was disappointment in Eli's voice. Luke hated

to cut the kid's ride short. It was a chance for him to escape his problems for at least a little while.

The two of them had talked earlier about his dad's drinking—about life, its hurts, its disappointments and expectations.

But now Luke had to get back.

He had a few of his own emotions to sort out.

Luke purred the bike to a stop at the back of the house. Eli slipped off the seat, and took off the helmet Luke had insisted he wear even though their ride was short.

"I appreciate your help with the bike," Luke said, taking back the helmet and hooking it behind the Harley's second seat. "If it weren't for you, I'd still be staring at the pieces of the front wheel and wondering what to do with them."

Eli smiled broadly. "Thank *you* for letting me help. And…and the ride was way cool. I'd never been on a Harley before."

"You have now, champ." He gave the kid a pat on the shoulder. "And don't forget about that repair shop one day. I just may need your services again."

"I won't."

Luke reached in his pocket and handed the boy a few bills. "For your services, my friend."

Eli looked down at the money and a wide smile spread across his face. *"Thanks!"*

"Consider it your first earnings on that future career of yours," Luke added.

The kid grinned like Luke had just promised him the world. Luke remembered feeling that way once.

Before his world had come crashing down.

He hoped the kid fared better.

* * *

Mariah knew Luke was gone.

She could sense the void in the very air around her.

His motorcycle was missing—and if she checked the cabin, she knew she'd find it empty. Not a sign that he'd ever been there.

But she couldn't bring herself to go and check.

She'd thought the tears would come—but they didn't. All she felt was an overwhelming sense of emptiness. She'd just lost the best man she would ever know.

She let out a desolate sigh and put supper on the table for Callie and her. She'd fixed extra—for Luke.

But she knew he wouldn't be here.

"I thought we'd have ice cream for dessert tonight," she said to Callie, a feeble attempt to brighten their solitary dinner.

"With chocolate sprinkles?"

"With chocolate sprinkles. If you eat everything on your plate," she added.

Callie chattered away all through dinner. Mariah was relieved she didn't ask about Luke. At least until she could decide how best to tell her he was gone.

Callie would be upset, not understanding that it had to be this way, that if Luke hadn't left today, he'd have left tomorrow.

Or the next day.

To a little girl, a few more days meant a lot.

Maybe they did to Mariah, as well.

After dinner she cleared the table, determined to go about her evening routine as if nothing was wrong, as if life was normal and her heart wasn't aching.

Callie played with her dolls, then it was bathtime, storytime and finally lights out. When her daughter had drifted off to sleep, Mariah gave her a soft kiss on the forehead—and slipped quietly from the bedroom.

Callie was her priority, she reminded herself. Her daughter was what mattered. Not Mariah's heartache over something that couldn't be.

But that realization didn't make her feel any better.

Nor miss Luke any less.

The rest of the night stretched out in front of her. So did the rest of her life, she thought, choking back the lump in her throat. She picked up the toys Callie had left lying about, then stole outdoors for a few quiet moments in the porch swing.

She hated the quiet. At least, she did tonight. The moon, every star, seemed to mock her. She wished Luke was here, that they could sit and talk about everything and nothing, that he'd lean close and brush her lips with his.

One more kiss, one more caress, one more night with him.

But that, she knew, would not happen. Nor would it help her pain; it would only postpone it.

His face came to her mind, that strong jaw, his smile that could destroy her senses and turn her legs to Jell-O, his soulful blue eyes that carried shadows of a pain Mariah could only imagine.

Her herbs had healed his cuts and bruises—but what would heal the pain in his soul?

Off in the distance she heard the yip of a coyote calling to its mate, then another sound—the rumble of a cycle.

Luke?

Her breath hung in her throat, unable to make it to her lungs. Her pulse scampered and her heart lurched. She stood, trying to see through the darkness.

The cycle pulled into the driveway and its noise quieted. She could see him. He was dressed in dark clothes, blending in with the night. Her stomach knotted and her heart clenched.

He took a few steps toward her, then stopped.

Luke didn't know why he'd turned back.

Maybe it was because he hadn't said goodbye to Mariah and Callie. Maybe he needed the peace of this place a little while longer. He didn't know—but something had pulled him back.

He saw Mariah holding on to a porch column as if it were a mast in the wind. The creamy moonlight illuminated her curves, outlined her features.

He thought he saw the glistening of tears in her eyes, but it could be a trick of the moonlight—he couldn't be sure.

Had she been missing him, the way he'd been missing her?

For days he'd itched to be on his way, to ride until fatigue overtook him. Now, when he could leave, something beckoned him to stay. Or rather, *someone*.

Mariah.

"I was, uh, wondering if I can use the cabin for a little while longer."

She studied him long and hard, as if deciding whether to say yes or no. "Is—is your leg hurting again?" she asked finally.

He considered lying, telling her yes, but feared that might get him another of her dangerous herbal treatments—at least dangerous to his libido.

And he wasn't sure he had the control right now.

He swallowed hard at the sight of her beauty and the way she made his pulse leap. "No," he said. "It's fine."

She tightened her hold on the porch support. "You left without saying goodbye."

It wasn't an accusation, but more a statement, as if she couldn't understand the reason.

Hell, he couldn't understand it, either. "I—I didn't know how, didn't know what to say."

She nodded her head, as if that made some kind of strange sense.

"I'm glad it isn't your leg," she said quietly. Finally she added, "The cabin is yours—if you want it."

He didn't feel he'd won any match. Mariah wouldn't turn away man or beast. It wasn't her nature. "Is everything all right? You? Callie?" he asked.

"We're fine," she said, then turned to go indoors.

"Mariah…?"

She stopped and turned.

"Thanks."

Luke didn't know what else to say, didn't know if there *was* anything else to say. And in the end, it didn't gain him any ground. Mariah only gave him a long, considering gaze, then turned and disappeared inside.

She was upset and he couldn't blame her. He shouldn't have left the way he had, without a goodbye, without even a thank-you.

She deserved better than that.

And it was something Luke had to remedy.

* * *

Luke would only be here for a while, she reminded herself. She hadn't known what to say to him. She understood why he hadn't been able to say goodbye. Mariah hadn't liked it, thought she deserved at least that—but she understood, too.

Goodbyes were hard.

Goodbyes were painful.

Maybe she should have sent him on his way. They could only complicate each other's lives. But she wasn't strong enough.

Not yet.

She didn't know why he'd come back—or if it would have been better if he'd kept on going. He'd found at least a small amount of peace while he was here.

She'd like to think he'd returned because of her, that he couldn't bear to leave her, that he'd discovered he loved her, the way she loved him. But she knew that was wishful thinking on her part.

Luke had no future here.

And Mariah had no future with him.

If she intended to grow stronger, if she intended to be able to say goodbye when the time came to do so, she had to resist temptation, had to resist Luke.

She had to think of what was best for her.

And for Callie.

She poured some of her calming herbal oil into her big, old-fashioned tub. The oil was one of the new herbal concoctions she'd mixed up for mail order.

It would get a definite test trial tonight, she thought as she sank into the bathwater and tried to relax.

After ten minutes she knew the oil was a failure. Or

maybe she was the failure. Her mind couldn't rid itself of the image of Luke standing there in the moonlight tonight, looking so very male, so tempting.

She'd wanted to run to him, throw her arms around his neck and let him absorb her into his heat, his strength. She wanted to make love with him—even if he'd be gone the next morning.

But that would not make her strong.

It would only make her weak.

Where had her usual good judgment gone? Mariah climbed out of the tub and wrapped a thick towel around herself, then turned to look at herself in the mirror.

She *looked* like the same woman, but she knew that inside she was different. Luke had turned her into someone she didn't know. A woman on the edge. A woman who could easily throw everything to the wind for a night in a man's arms.

Who are you? And what have you done with Mariah Cade? she asked the image.

Luke ran with the kite, letting its bright colors soar in the clear blue sky the next afternoon.

"Let me, let me," Callie sang as she chased after him.

"Okay, let's see what you can do." He put the string in Callie's small hand and helped her run.

"I'm doing it. I'm doing it. Look at me, Mommy," she called out to Mariah.

Mariah had come outdoors to watch her daughter. Luke tried to keep his mind on kite-flying and his young protégée—and off her pretty mother.

The air currents shifted and the kite came floating down, landing on a nearby bush.

"Oh, no," Callie screeched. She gave a quick glance at Luke and her small face puckered.

"It's okay, princess. A kite floats on the wind, and when there's no wind, the kite comes down," he explained, thus saving a few tears.

"But I want to see it fly."

"I want to see it fly, too. But first I have to rescue it from that bush. Are there any thorns on it?"

"No—roses have thorns. That's one of Mommy's butterfly bushes."

"Butterfly bush?" Luke had never heard of such a thing. "Does it grow butterflies?"

"No, silly—the butterflies like it, so they go around it."

"Ohhhhh." Luke drew out the word and noticed the threat of tears had faded. "Then it doesn't eat kites?"

She giggled. "That's silly. A bush can't eat a kite."

Luke smiled. "They just eat butterflies."

She swiveled her head from side to side. "They don't eat butterflies, either. Don't you know anything?"

"Just how to make little girls giggle. Come on, let's go rescue it."

He spent a few minutes untangling string from the small purple blooms. The kite itself looked intact, ready to fly again. If there was wind.

Which there wasn't.

Not a wisp.

Luke made an exaggerated show of wetting his finger and holding it up in the air, checking for any. "No wind, I'm afraid. The next air launch will have to wait."

"O-kay," she said reluctantly.

Luke glanced over at Mariah and caught her laughing at their exchange. She looked truly beautiful, the sun glistening on her tanned skin, the laughter brightening her green eyes, her denim shorts showing a lot of leg. He could spend the rest of his life just looking at her, he thought.

He sauntered over and sat down beside her on the ground.

"Okay—what's so funny?" he asked.

She smiled and it lit up her face. "You."

"I'm funny?"

"Bushes that eat kites and butterflies?"

"Could happen."

"I love to see her like this, running and playing…like a normal child."

Her voice sounded wistful and Luke knew her heart was breaking for her daughter.

"I've been thinking," he said. "Callie would really benefit from a swing and an old-fashioned jungle gym."

The suggestion brightened her face for a quick moment, then she turned solemn. "I've thought about that—but they cost and arm and a leg."

"Not if I build it. Is there a lumberyard anywhere near here?"

"You build things?" she asked.

"I'm a versatile man."

He was all man, she thought. Along with funny, intelligent, warm, sexy. The sexy part caught on her brain cells and she couldn't finish the list.

"The lumberyard," he said, bringing her back to the conversation.

"Luke, that's a lot of work—and expense, too."

"Let me worry about that."

She read his face. His eyes were the blue of the sky

overhead, intent. He meant it; he wanted to do this for Callie. She glanced over at her daughter, who was pretending to be a kite, twirling and spinning in the warm summer sun.

She would benefit, as Luke said. And she'd absolutely love it. "There's Johnson's Lumber. It's a small place about ten miles out of town."

"Good. Can I take your truck in the morning?"

Mariah knew it would keep Luke here longer.

And that wasn't good for her heart.

"Yes," she said. "If you're sure you want to do this."

Chapter Twelve

Over the following week Luke worked on the swing set for Callie. He'd taken Mariah's truck and hauled home the treated lumber from Johnson's. It was an odd little place outside town, and old man Johnson apparently didn't have enough to keep him occupied because he followed Luke around, talking his ear off.

But Luke hadn't minded, because when he'd told the guy he was building a play set for Callie Cade so she could exercise her weakened joints, he'd thrown in all the nails and bolts gratis. And, Luke suspected, given him a discount on the lumber.

He worked his buns off during the day so that, when nightfall came, he'd be too damned tired and sore to even *think* about seducing Mariah.

Callie had supervised the construction job, holding the hammer or drill for him as needed. Eli had pitched in to help, as well, though this job probably wasn't nearly as appealing to him as working on Luke's cycle.

Mariah hadn't asked him why he'd come back, but at odd moments he'd caught her gaze on him, as if she had questions. Luke wasn't sure he'd have the answers, had she asked.

He tried to tell himself that he owed her, owed everyone for their kindness and generosity. But he knew deep down there was more to why he'd come back than that.

He found Mariah as tempting as all get-out, but that, he knew, was lust. Lust had never kept him this intrigued before. Lust wouldn't have dragged him back when he'd ridden eighty miles down the highway in the hot Arizona sun.

Don't think about it too closely, his head told him.

Each noon Mariah had insisted he take a break and have lunch. They would either picnic by the stream or sit around Mariah's kitchen table. A few evenings Luke had taken them for pizza, even though he'd had to endure the curious looks and questions of the locals wondering why he was still around—and, no doubt, thinking that things between him and Mariah were serious.

Serious! Luke had done little more than kiss her on the cheek one night. That had been enough to fire up his hormones and he hadn't tried it since.

"Luke, this is terrific," Mariah said as he put the finishing touches on the exercise part of the play set.

Luke showed her how Callie could use it to exercise and how it could be adjusted, notch after notch, as she grew older.

Tears came to Mariah's eyes. She couldn't help it. No man had ever done anything this nice for her before, or been so supportive of Callie. Luke had understood her daughter's needs and worked to make things better.

"This will help her so much," she said.

"Not as much as you do, Mariah—with your herbs and your healing. Callie is thriving."

"Thank you." She brushed away her tears. She hated to cry—especially in front of Luke, but she was overwhelmed by his thoughtfulness.

"All it needs now is the swing. Old man Johnson didn't have the materials, so I thought I'd go to Cottonwood this afternoon and see what I can find there."

"This afternoon?"

"Yes—why? Is that a problem?"

"No, I was just thinking we might go with you. Callie's been doing well lately, and if we don't stay long, she'd love the outing."

Luke was surprised. Mariah was usually so protective of her daughter. But she was right—Callie had been doing well lately. They'd take it slow and easy on the drive. And if there was enough daylight left when they got home he'd install the swing.

He couldn't remember anything he'd done that felt more rewarding. And Callie deserved it. She was one valiant little girl.

And so was her mother.

"I'd like that," he said. "And I promise I'll miss all the potholes."

He'd enjoy having them along on the ride. It would help pass the time. Of course, being with Mariah for the afternoon carried its own set of problems. But Luke could handle the temptation.

He hoped.

Besides, having Callie in the seat between them would keep him circumspect. He had no idea why he'd come back—but he did know he couldn't complicate Mariah's life when he didn't even know where his own was going.

Maybe she should have tossed him out on his ear, especially after he'd seduced her that night by the stream. But she hadn't. And Luke couldn't take advantage of her friendship—or whatever this crazy thing was between them.

He was a man with no future, a man who'd once had it all. Med school, head of a trauma center—it had all been his for the asking. But when Dane had died, literally beneath his well-trained hands, he found he had nothing.

The trip there and back had gone well. Luke had taken the road at a sedate pace, and they'd stopped occasionally to let Callie stretch her arms and legs.

Luke had found a hardware store that had everything he needed for the swing, and they'd stopped at a fast food restaurant for a quick dinner before leaving Cottonwood.

Mariah had enjoyed the afternoon—and so had Callie, though she'd fallen asleep on the ride home.

Luke pulled the old truck into her long driveway and parked it at the back, then helped her get her tired child into the house.

They'd just stepped inside when Una pounded on the back door and bustled in, looking upset and frightened.

"What is it, Una?" Mariah asked.

"I'll go put Callie down and be right back," Luke said.

Mariah watched him head for the bedroom, then turned back to Una. "What's wrong?"

"There's been an accident."

Una could barely catch her breath. Mariah tried to get her to sit, but the woman was too riled up.

"Who—Eli? Jimmy?" she asked.

"Jimmy. The Henios just called me. He's been drinking again—and wrecked his truck on that big curve out by their place."

Mariah knew the place she meant. It had always been a bad spot, but the county never had the funds to do the roadwork necessary to make that stretch safer.

"Is he hurt?"

"I don't know—they just said it looked…bad. They called the ambulance and the sheriff, but neither has gotten there yet. I'm so worried. And Eli is upset."

Tears rolled down the woman's face and Mariah turned to Luke. She'd heard him enter the kitchen. Her neighbor was distraught. And Mariah needed his help.

"I heard," he said.

She turned to Una. "Luke will go—if Jimmy's badly hurt—"

"No, Mariah—"

She turned back to Luke—and found his face set in stony resolve. "But, Luke, you're a doctor. You've done this kind of thing before. You'll know what to do, how to help."

She was worried for Una, for Eli. And right now they could use his skills. He couldn't say no. But he brushed past her and disappeared out the back door.

Mariah didn't know what to do.

She got Una a glass of water and insisted she sit down. "Luke will go," she said again, though she no longer believed the words.

This time Una obeyed and collapsed onto a kitchen chair. Mariah set the water in front of her. She needed to find Luke.

Mariah spotted him in the yard, pacing restlessly. "Luke—"

The haunted shadows were back in his eyes. A muscle ticked along his jawline. "Mariah—let the paramedics handle it. Don't ask me."

His voice was cold—and she didn't know if she could reach him. His son's death had taken a cruel toll on him, tearing apart who and what he was.

"This isn't Chicago, Luke. We don't have paramedics on every corner. They come from a distance—over bad roads. You're a doctor—and you're closer. If Jimmy is badly hurt—"

"You don't understand, Mariah. I left medicine because I had to— I saw Dane's face on every patient they brought in, every patient I couldn't save. I…had to watch him die again and again. And—" His voice broke. "And I couldn't do it anymore. I *can't* do it anymore."

"Oh, Luke—"

"I don't want any damned sympathy, Mariah. I just want to be left alone."

And let all his talents go to waste?

Mariah didn't believe in wasting anything. Especially a life. "You have my sympathy about your son, Luke, but not about the career you're determined to throw away. You're a doctor…you *could* make a difference tonight—and you won't."

Mariah hated to lose her temper. She seldom did. And right now she wasn't feeling very good about it. Luke was hurting—and she'd hit him pretty hard.

"I won't ask again." She turned, feeling every bit of her defeat—and saw Eli standing there.

But Eli wasn't looking at her; his gaze was on Luke.

"You're a doctor," he said, his voice low, accusatory. "I thought doctors *helped* people."

Luke met his steely gaze. It skewered into him. And he felt like he couldn't breathe. "There's nothing I can do," he said.

His words were harsh and Eli looked like he'd just been slapped. He saw the boy's shoulders slump, saw the disappointment in his eyes before he turned and loped toward home.

"Damn—damn it all to hell," Luke said, hating himself, seeing his failure reflected in Eli's eyes.

Seeing it reflected in Mariah's, as well.

That was the part that hurt.

"Okay," he said. He could do it this one last time, do it for Mariah. "I'll go."

Red flashing lights lit the night sky. It was the sheriff's car arriving at the scene. Luke pulled the truck in next to it and jumped out.

"*You*—stay back," the sheriff commanded.

"Dr. Luke Phillips, Sheriff," Luke said. "I'm a trauma doctor."

"Then come with me. Let's see what we got. Damn drunks," he cursed beneath his breath.

Luke winced. He wished he'd had a heart-to-heart with Jimmy, told him to get his sorry butt to the closest AA meeting—or Luke would drag him there himself, kicking and screaming. It might've prevented this.

From the looks of the scene, it was a one-vehicle

accident. At least Jimmy hadn't taken out another car, he thought.

But it was a small consolation.

"Looks like he rolled two or three times," the sheriff said, his mood not any less surly. "Help me get him out."

Jimmy was pinned beneath the steering wheel, the truck on its top. "Sheriff, if there's no threat of explosion, let me check for vitals and cord damage first," he said, wishing like hell he was anywhere else but here.

Why had he agreed to do this?

"The damn truck doesn't look like it ever had more than five gallons of gas in it at any one time. Probably not enough to explode. Have at it."

Luke hadn't treated a patient in over two months—and he didn't want to treat this one, either. He'd quit, walked away from that life.

Mariah shouldn't have asked him to do this. The memories were too fresh, the pain still sharp.

He checked for a carotid pulse and found one. At least Jimmy was alive. Now the trick was to keep him that way.

He checked reflexes. A little slow, but spinal column hopefully intact. "Okay to move him, Sheriff—but let's be cautious of the spine anyway."

How many Jimmys had he seen come through the trauma unit?

Many he'd been able to save, some he had not. He thought of Eli, the anger in the kid's eyes. He thought of Mariah and the bald belief she had in him. Well, there were no guarantees in medicine.

Why the hell hadn't he kept on riding? Why had he turned back? Now he'd gotten himself involved in something that could very well destroy what was left of him.

Another patrol car arrived just then and the deputy rushed up carrying a blanket and standard first-aid kit.

"He's shocky—let's put him down here. Get the blanket on him."

Luke's instincts kicked in now—but it did damn little to eradicate the fear. Bile rose up to choke him.

He raised Jimmy's legs to keep the blood pumping to vital organs. The blanket would help conserve body heat and hopefully prevent deeper shock.

He nodded to the deputy. "Hold his legs so I can check him. Where the hell is that ambulance? We need to transport *now*."

"Uh—it's held up on another call. We only got one ambulance to cover this area," the deputy said, but he took over, freeing Luke to check the gushing head wound.

Luke stanched the flow of the pumper with everything he could find in the first-aid kit. Head wounds often looked worse than they were. But there could be bleeding inside the brain. Luke thought it a strong possibility.

He was certain there were cracked ribs and he had to fear lung collapse. Damn—it was like working with both hands tied behind his back. Luke had no IV fluids, no plasma, no meds—and he didn't hear the distant sound of an ambulance riding to his rescue.

Sweat beaded his forehead. Luke prayed this wasn't a patient he'd see Dane's face in, that he wouldn't have to watch his son die all over again.

"This guy needs a hospital. How far to the nearest trauma unit?"

"Hell, Doc," the sheriff said. "We're out in the sticks. There *ain't* no trauma unit."

"I'll settle for a hospital—you have one of those?"

"It's twenty miles."

Luke cursed silently. "We'll use your car. Let's load him in the back—and, Sheriff, lights and sirens."

They got Jimmy into the backseat, and Luke stayed with him, keeping the legs elevated above his heart and monitoring his thready pulse.

The sheriff drove like the devil was chasing him, and Jimmy gave an audible groan when they hit a good-size pothole. Okay—he was feeling something.

Luke drew in a breath.

It was a good sign, but he didn't kid himself. Jimmy was in a bad way.

"Call ahead to the hospital," he told the sheriff. "Tell them our ETA and that we have a possible brain injury, collapsed lung and internal damage. Patient comatose and in shock. Tell them to have X-ray standing by and a surgeon, preferably neuro. And see if they can scare up anyone trained in trauma."

Luke doubted he'd get trauma help or a neurosurgeon, but it didn't hurt to ask. "Barring that, see if they can get a medivac here. We may have to fly him to Phoenix."

Luke worked by rote—but if this case went south Luke would have a price to pay later when the night's events came crashing in on him.

When memories of Dane, memories of Luke's failure that night in Chicago, hit full-blast.

Luke had promised himself he'd never be put in this position again, never be responsible for another person's life. But here he was, enmeshed in something he shouldn't be, all because one beautiful woman believed he could walk on water.

What she didn't realize was that Luke could fail.

Again. And if he did, there would be nothing left of him but a cold, empty shell.

The way it had been when his son had died.

Mariah paced the small kitchen. She thought Luke would have called by now. Una and Eli were beside themselves with worry. Mariah tried to calm them, but she was worried about Jimmy, too.

She was also worried about Luke.

Had she asked too much of him? She'd seen the agony in his face, knew he wasn't ready to return to medicine—and perhaps never would be. Oh, Luke! she thought. She hadn't been willing to listen to him, to understand his pain.

He must hate her.

And if Jimmy didn't make it…

What would that do to Luke?

Just then the phone rang, startling them all. Una and Eli eyed the thing like it was a viper ready to strike. Mariah answered. It wasn't Luke. It was a nurse from the hospital. They were bringing Jimmy in just then. No, she didn't know any particulars. She'd just been asked to call.

Probably by Luke, Mariah thought.

She wanted to ask what was happening, if Luke was okay. But that would be ridiculous. Jimmy was the patient—not Luke. Still, Luke was the one on her mind.

"I want to go to the hospital," Una said, standing up. "I want to see Jimmy." Then she reeled on her feet.

Mariah helped her back into her seat.

"I want to go, too," Eli said.

"We'll all go," Mariah told them. "Luke has my

truck. I'll have to drive your car, Una. Just let me find a neighbor to watch Callie."

"Call Mrs. Charley," Una said. "I'm sure she'll be happy to help out."

A short while later they were on the road.

No one spoke. Their thoughts were all on Jimmy— and what they'd find when they reached the hospital. Mariah hoped Luke had been able to make a difference. She had asked him to do the impossible.

It was so very soon after his son's death.

Was he up to the shock?

The horrible reminders?

Mariah prayed that he was—and sent silent words of encouragement his way.

She loved him, suspected she had from the very first day she met him. And that love had only increased every day since.

He'd walked through a hell no man should ever have to go through. His was a battered soul, and Mariah wished she could heal him, heal him with caring, with her love.

Could she do that before he left here? Could she say goodbye to him and send him back to what he was meant to do? Return to medicine?

Or by asking him to help tonight, had she ruined any chance of Luke ever being whole again?

The drive seemed to take forever—and then some. But they finally reached the hospital. Jimmy was still in the emergency room. No one could tell them anything yet about his condition, just that the doctors were with him.

Una's eyes took on a haunted look as she sat outside the E.R. doors, her shoulders shaking, her hands trembling in her lap.

She looked like she'd aged tonight.

And Mariah was furious with Jimmy for not seeing what he was doing to his family.

Eli paced the hallway, hands jammed into his pockets, worry etching his face. It had only been a year and a half ago that Eli's mother had died in this same hospital, died from a chance blood clot. She knew Eli had to be remembering. And now he had to fear losing his father.

Mariah worried for the boy's mental state. She worried for Una. *And* hoped this wouldn't be more bad news for this little family.

Luke was exhausted as he walked out of the E.R. The modest hospital had no trauma-trained personnel, but had quickly cut through red tape and granted him consult status, enabling him to treat his patient.

Luke had excused himself once he had Jimmy stabilized. The man would make it—but it had been dicey for a while. Now all Luke felt was fatigue. He was too damned tired to even feel good about saving the man's life.

There'd been no sign of brain swelling, but Jimmy had several fractured ribs, a collapsed lung and bruised internal organs. One leg had sustained a bad fracture, as well. In a day or two he'd need surgery to repair his femur, but for now Luke's patient was both conscious and lucky.

Luke glanced up and saw Mariah. He should have known she couldn't sit and wait at home. Nor could Una or Eli, as it turned out.

They were all there, but Mariah was the one who held his attention. Her face was pale, her small shoulders tense, but she looked beautiful to him. She was consoling Una. Always the healer, Luke thought.

In retrospect, everything he'd done tonight paled in comparison to her. She had the rare talent of comforting, of healing whomever was in need—with no thought to herself.

Eli was pacing the hall like a boy possessed. When he spotted Luke he came running up. "How's my dad?"

His young face beseeched him.

Luke was relieved he had positive news to give, instead of the opposite. "I was just about to give a report to your grandmother. Let's go over there."

Eli's eyes darkened with fear. Luke tried to force a smile to make the boy relax, let him know everything was going to be all right, but he didn't have any smiles at the ready.

He hadn't forgotten how difficult tonight had been.

Hadn't forgotten that it could just as easily have turned out badly.

Una glanced up as they approached. He saw the worry, the pleading in her eyes. Mariah's gaze was glued to him, worry limning her face.

"How is my son?" Una asked.

"He's going to make it," Luke said.

Una stood up and threw her arms around his neck. "I knew you'd help my Jimmy."

Eli seemed to lose his earlier anger at Luke. And Mariah was all smiles.

He gave a layman's rundown of the injuries Jimmy had sustained and what he still had to face: surgery for his fractured leg and Alcoholics Anonymous. If Jimmy didn't sober up and stay sober he was another accident waiting to happen.

His family agreed.

"Can we see him?" Una asked.

"They're finishing with him now, then they'll be wheeling him to his room. You can walk along with the gurney when they move him."

Una collapsed onto the chair she'd been sitting on and Eli sank down beside her.

Luke turned to Mariah. "You wouldn't happen to know where I could get a cup of coffee, would you?"

"I would," she answered. "I got one for Una a short while ago. Follow me."

Mariah wanted to give Eli and Una time alone with Jimmy and she could use some coffee herself. They had a thirty-mile drive home to make. "We'll be in the cafeteria," she told Una.

She started down the hallway with Luke. He fit here, she realized. In a hospital. It was his realm. Whether he went back to Chicago now, or after some hard soul-searching, she knew she would lose him. He would return to medicine.

Whether he knew it yet or not.

They reached the cafeteria. The place was closed this time of night, except for the coffee bar, which stayed open twenty-four hours.

When they had their drinks they sat down at a small table. Mariah wrapped her hands around her cup for warmth, and maybe strength. She was quiet for a moment, realizing he didn't want to talk about tonight. The shadows weren't there in his eyes—just a certain weariness.

"As soon as Una and Eli have a moment with Jimmy we can start home. A neighbor is watching Callie, and I don't want to impose on her too long."

She was babbling, she knew, not knowing how to ask the question that was on her mind: *How was he?*

Her gaze coursed over him. He looked good, so very good. Her Luke. But he wasn't her Luke. He belonged to something bigger than himself, bigger than her, than the two of them.

And the realization brought tears to her eyes.

Luke misinterpreted them. "Jimmy doesn't deserve your tears, Mariah," he said. "Not with what his drinking has put everybody through."

Quickly she reached up and brushed them away. "They're not for Jimmy," she said.

He studied her for a long, quiet moment. "Then who?"

She didn't want to answer. His gaze was penetrating, and she felt he could see right into her heart. "Something silly," she answered.

He took her hand, then turned it over and kissed her open palm. "Tell me."

She jerked her hand away. The kiss he'd planted there had made her tingle all over, made her realize how very much she wanted him—a man she couldn't have. "For you, for me...for us."

"And that makes you cry? Us?"

"I told you it was silly." She jumped up from her chair. "Let's go see if Eli and Una are ready to leave."

Luke stood up, but before Mariah could turn to leave, he took her arm, essentially pinning her to the spot. "Mariah..." He tipped up her chin and kissed her lips.

Heat rippled through her and she melded to him, fitting against him as if they were one entity, as if together they could solve anything—but Mariah knew that wasn't true.

Soon, too soon, she would have to say goodbye to him.

Chapter Thirteen

It was three o'clock in the morning when Luke drove them all home. Una was less anxious after seeing Jimmy, but the night had been a terrible strain for her. Eli had fallen asleep in the backseat soon after they'd left the hospital, unable to stay awake any longer.

It had been a long, frightening night for all of them.

Mariah thanked Mrs. Charley for coming to stay with Callie, then went to the bedroom to peek in on her daughter and found her sleeping soundly.

"How is she?" Luke asked as she came out of Callie's room.

"She's fast asleep—snuggled up with one of her stuffed animals.

She took down two goblets from the cabinet and poured white wine into each, then handed one to Luke.

He was easily the most handsome man she'd ever met, but he was also the most complicated.

Almost as if she didn't know him at all.

And yet, in many ways, she felt as if she'd always known him.

One thing Mariah knew, the title "doctor" fit him. She had seen that tonight at the hospital. It was where he belonged—and that knowledge made her heart ache.

She took a small sip of wine, and felt its effects seep into her tense muscles.

They took their glasses out to the front porch, to soak up the night air and the solitude. Mariah sat on the top step instead of the swing, certain she didn't need the swaying motion mingling with the effects of the wine.

So far her drink hadn't done much in the way of relaxation. Her neck felt taut as a bowstring, as if it would snap if she moved it. And it was beginning to give her a headache of gigantic proportions, as well.

She reached back to try to massage away the tight knots, hoping for some relief. Maybe she would take a long, hot bath before bed and sprinkle in some of her lavender oil.

"Stiff neck?" Luke asked.

"Just a little," she admitted. "I guess tonight was more stressful than I realized."

In more ways than one, Luke thought, remembering his own qualms and uncertainties. But there would be time to reflect on that later. The night's experience had left him with serious questions, questions he knew he had to think through.

Decisions he needed to make.

He sat down next to Mariah on the porch step and

took her wineglass, setting it aside, along with his own. "Scoot back here against me, and let me see what I can do to relax your neck muscles," he said.

"Oh, Luke—you don't have to do that. I'll be fine. It's just a little tension." She gave her neck a final rub.

"Aha—so that's it," he said. "The healer can dish out treatment, but can't take it herself."

Before she could say another word, his hands were at work on her neck and shoulders, finding all the painful spots. She gave a soft moan at his touch, the strength of his fingers as they worked to knead the pain, the tension, from her little by little.

"Now, isn't that better?" he asked.

"Better than better."

His fingers worked her taut muscles, and she leaned back into his touch, wanting more. Her eyes closed— and she felt herself floating on a wave of pure relief.

This was better than the hot lavender bath she'd planned on.

If only she could bottle those hands of his, she thought with a smile, she could make a mint.

She shouldn't let herself get too used to this, her brain reminded. Luke wasn't here to stay. But she shoved the thought aside. She wanted to enjoy the short time she had left with Luke.

All too soon he would ride out of her life—either on his way to nowhere, a lost soul, a lone man searching for escape from himself, or back to where he came from. And either way, she would lose him.

He planted a kiss on a tender spot on her shoulder— and Mariah felt the heat flood through her, melting the knot away, seeping deep into her bones.

His mouth was magic, finding each tight place, his warm breath a velvet whisper against her skin. He dropped a trail of kisses on her neck, along her shoulder, then her collarbone.

Mariah didn't know a collarbone could be an erogenous zone.

But Luke had found a way to make it one.

She gave a small groan of pleasure as he turned her in his arms and his mouth found hers.

"Mariah…" He murmured her name against her lips, and she drank in the sound, loving it, loving *him*.

She'd tried so hard not to let it happen. But it had. Her world spun, a little cockeyed, a little shaky, but definitely dizzying.

He drew back, his gaze warm on her, his eyes a languid blue in the moonlight, and she saw in them the same agony that had to be there in her own—a need that shouldn't be, a need that could be satisfied, but would take them nowhere.

"Feel better now?" he asked. His voice was low and thick with want.

"Yes." She tried a smile, felt it wobble on her lips, then put her hands to his handsome face, framing it between them, her mind memorizing every angle and plane of it, branding the sight of him onto her brain.

Because soon that's all she would have.

Luke had tossed and turned in fitful sleep that night. Intermingled with thoughts of Mariah were thoughts of what he knew he had to do. If he was ever going to reclaim his life, he needed to go back and face his fears.

Last night his emergency instincts had kicked in. Medicine had felt good again. He had been in control. All his fears had receded.

But what if Jimmy had died? Would that have sent him plummeting into that old darkness? Back into his fears? His doubts? Aware of his failure that awful night that Dane had died.

He had no answers to those questions.

Nor did he have answers to the question of Mariah.

It had taken every ounce of his willpower to pull away from her last night, not to take her to the cabin and into his bed.

Her kisses had been hot and sultry, her body warm, receptive. She'd made him feel good—whole again. In a way he hadn't felt in a long while.

He had a lot to wrestle with in his mind, feelings he needed to sort out. In the meantime he had to get Mariah's truck home from the accident site. Una had promised to watch Callie while he and Mariah went to retrieve it.

It was barely sunup when he appeared at her back door, early for breakfast, but he couldn't endure the bed—or his thoughts—a moment longer.

Mariah was baking cinnamon rolls. She looked so fresh, so beautiful, his heart slammed against his ribs at the sight of her.

She smiled as he stepped into the kitchen—and Luke wanted to taste her again, finish what he'd started last night. But that, he knew, wasn't a good idea.

"You look tired," she said as she poured a glass of fresh-squeezed orange juice and handed it to him. "Have a seat. The coffee should be ready soon."

"Thanks," he said for the juice. "Is there anything I can do?"

She dropped a pair of pot holders in front of him. "I need to help Callie get dressed and into her braces. If the timer goes off, take the cinnamon rolls out of the oven, okay?"

He nodded. "I think I can handle that."

A short while later everyone had gathered around the small kitchen table—Una, Callie, Mariah and himself. Eli, Una had said, was still asleep. Last night had been hard for him.

Luke poured coffee for everyone and a glass of milk for Callie.

After they'd finished with breakfast, he and Mariah took off.

"We won't be long," she called over her shoulder to Una.

"Don't worry about a thing. Callie and I are going to read a story this morning," she answered.

"I'm so lucky to have her," Mariah said as she followed Luke to the cycle.

"And I think Una's lucky to have you for a friend."

Mariah studied the bike, their transportation out to the accident site. "Where do I sit? On that little seat?"

A smiled curved at Luke's mouth. "You've never been on a cycle before?"

Should she have? He said it like she'd missed out on a life experience. "Never."

"Then you're in for an adventure."

Mariah climbed onto the seat behind him. She searched around for handholds, but couldn't find any. "What do I hang on to?"

"Me. Wrap your arms around my waist."

Mariah hesitated. Her arms around Luke's midsection didn't seem like the best idea at the moment. She was all too aware of the man as it was. Then he started the engine—and Mariah grabbed hold fast.

"Hang on tight," he said.

As if she could do anything but, she thought, as Luke sped down the driveway. She clung even tighter to him as he reached the road and increased his speed.

Her heart raced as fast as the cycle, and the created wind stole her breath.

"You okay?" he screamed over his shoulder.

Was she? She hugged the hard muscles of his back and refused to open her eyes. She didn't want to see death coming. Why had she agreed to this?

They could have just as easily borrowed Una's car, and Mariah sorely wished they had.

"I'm fine," she said. At least she hoped she was. How was she supposed to know? She grabbed a handful of his blue denim shirt and held on for dear life. "How much farther?" she shouted over the noise.

"You tell me—you live here."

"Can't," she said.

"Can't?"

"I'd have to open my eyes."

A hearty laugh rumbled through him. Mariah could feel it as she hugged his back. "It isn't funny, Luke Phillips."

But he seemed to think it was. His laughter continued, the sound carried on the air. And Mariah had had enough. She pinched him—hard.

On that lean, flat, sexy stomach of his.

"Ow—that hurt," he bellowed.

At least his laughter stopped.

Finally they reached the curve where the wreck had happened. Luke pulled up next to her truck and Mariah slid off the cycle, happy to have her feet on solid ground again. "I will never, ever, get on a motorcycle again as long as I live," she said.

Luke saw she was trembling and her legs were wobbly. "Come here," he said.

She took a small half step forward, then stopped as if she was afraid to risk coming any closer. Maybe she thought he was still mad about that pinch of hers. She had a lot of strength in her fingers, he had to admit. She'd gotten his attention. And he'd found out she didn't like being laughed at.

He pulled her into his arms, holding her tight until the trembling had stopped. "You *were* frightened. I'm sorry, babe. I shouldn't have laughed at you."

"You shouldn't have. And I...shouldn't have pinched you," she allowed then. "I'm sorry."

He loved the feel of her in his arms, the way she'd burrowed into him. "Do you think you're able to drive the truck home?" he asked when she'd drawn away from him.

She nodded. "I'm fine," she said and her chin rose to a proud angle.

She wanted him to believe she was tough. And she was. She might not be at ease on a Harley, but she was one strong woman, one he admired.

He opened the truck door for her and she climbed inside.

"See you back at the house," he said, then watched as she drove off.

How would he ever be able to walk away from her?

* * *

Luke was working on Callie's swing. Mariah saw him from the kitchen window. She'd been busy with her herbs all afternoon, preparing and drying them, mixing and extracting their oil, but her mind was on the man in the backyard.

She'd sensed him wrestling with something all day, during the quick lunch she'd fixed them, and in pensive moments since.

She funneled lavender oil into small bottles, some for her mail orders, some for herself. Mariah loved its scent, knew its antiseptic and anti-inflammatory qualities.

She'd just finished attaching the last label when Luke walked in the back door.

"Is Callie awake?" he asked. "The swing is finished."

Mariah glanced at the kitchen clock. "Quiet time is over. I don't think she's slept. She's just been playing with her dolls. I'll go check and see."

Luke smelled the fresh, flowery scent of the oil Mariah had been working with. He lifted a bottle and sniffed. She'd used some of this stuff on his wounds, he remembered. But what he remembered most was her touch.

How would he ever forget it?

Just then Callie came bounding into the kitchen. "Is my swing all put t'gether?" she asked.

"It sure is, pretty miss," he said. "Ready to try it out?"

"Mmm-hmm!" She beat Luke to the back door, her pert little face all smiles.

He liked the smile on Mariah's face, as well.

"Luke, I don't know how to thank you for Callie's play set. It will be so wonderful for her."

"Glad I could help."

They followed Callie outside.

"Swing me, Luke," Callie said and raced to the play set, her little legs managing well.

Mariah enjoyed Callie's squeals of delight as Luke pushed her in the swing. She didn't know anything that could have pleased her child more. Or herself. It had been a gift for her, as well. Mariah could never have provided this for Callie.

"Why the tears?" Luke asked her a short while later. Callie was climbing on the gym he'd fashioned.

"I'm just being silly." Mariah waved off his question. "I'm just happy for what you did for her."

"Well, it's not worth crying over," he said, touching her cheek and brushing an errant tear away with the pad of his thumb.

His touch was electric, and she worked to rein in her feelings. "I—I told you I was being silly."

Luke needed a walk.

The swing set was finished and Luke had no more reason to stay here.

He found himself at the small stream at the back of Mariah's property. The place where he'd made love with her. Memories of that night hid in the later-afternoon shadows, threatening to jump out and swamp him.

He'd been struggling with thoughts of her, her sweetness and femininity, for the past two days. And opposite that, the increasing realization that he had to go back to Chicago, back to the E.R., if he was ever going to be whole again.

He shoved a hand through his hair and cursed to himself.

Could he leave here, leave Mariah and Callie and Sunrise? Leave this place, the beautiful red earth, the bad roads and all the solitude a man could want? Leave the woman who was the best thing that had ever happened to him?

He tossed a pebble into the stream and counted the ripples that ebbed away from it. His life at the moment was just as ephemeral, he thought to himself.

And he knew it was time to make a decision.

Mariah had Callie all ready for bed that night. Her daughter had been so excited over the play set, she wasn't sure she'd ever get her to sleep.

Luke had become a big hero in her daughter's eyes, someone larger than life, bigger than Santa Claus, the Easter Bunny and the Tooth Fairy all rolled into one.

And Mariah didn't know how to bring her down to earth.

Back to the reality that Luke would be leaving.

Nor did she know how to bring herself down to the same reality.

"Can Luke take me to my school when I start next month?" Callie asked exuberantly.

"Callie—" Mariah didn't know what to say. Tears filled her eyes.

"Mommy, don't cry. You can come, too."

Mariah had to smile. She tucked back a silky strand of hair from her child's forehead and placed her favorite stuffed animal beside her.

"If Luke is still here when you start school, we'll both take you," she said lamely and knew that wasn't the right answer to give. Luke would surely be gone by then. "Now, close your eyes and get to sleep."

She would have to explain to Callie that Luke would be leaving. In fact, she should have done it long before now. But Mariah had been postponing the inevitable.

For her own selfish reasons.

Her daughter snuggled down in the bed covers, and Mariah leaned over to kiss her forehead. "Good night, baby," she said.

"G'night, Mommy."

Quietly she turned out the light and slipped from the room.

With a heavy sigh she headed for the kitchen to fix herself a hot cup of chamomile tea, hoping it would quiet her troubled heart.

Luke found her there three cups later, when she was no closer to finding the calm she sought.

He rapped on the back door, then came into the kitchen.

"Can I fix you something?" she asked.

He shook his head. "I just came over to tell you I talked to Jimmy earlier this evening. I think the accident has sobered him in more ways than one. He's vowed no more drinking. And has agreed to attend AA meetings. At least it's a start."

"A good start. Oh, Luke I don't know how to thank you. For *everything* you've done for him and his family."

A smile curved her pretty lips, and Luke knew he was a coward. That wasn't the only thing he had come here to tell her. "Maybe I'll take some coffee. Any left?"

"On the counter, but it's not decaf."

Luke didn't care. He'd be up all night, anyway, too wired to sleep. "That's all right."

He poured a cup and joined her at the table.

How many times had he sat here, enjoying Mariah's company? Times too numerous to count. And this would be the last time. He had to go back to Chicago. Had to leave this little family, this very special woman.

"Mariah, I—" The words stuck in Luke's throat, and he couldn't say them. He'd rehearsed them a hundred times tonight.

"You're leaving. I know," she said, so quietly, so softly he barely heard her words.

He nodded. "You made me see what I need to do, that I have to go back if I'm ever going to be a whole person again. I can't keep on running. I had to face my fears the night of Jimmy's accident. I did it for you, Mariah— because I saw the disappointment in your eyes. I was afraid I'd fail Eli, you, Una, but mostly you. I couldn't bear that."

There was a lump in Mariah's throat the size of a watermelon—because she knew he was right.

"When...are you leaving?"

"In the morning. I want to say goodbye to Callie and to Eli and Una."

Callie. It would break her daughter's heart. It would also disappoint Eli—and Una. Una had such high hopes that Luke was the right man for Mariah.

She nodded numbly.

"I—I need to pack tonight."

It was so final—and Mariah felt her heart shatter. She'd wanted this for Luke. He could do so much good with his medicine. But it wasn't what she wanted for herself.

She wrapped her hands around her cup—but her tea had grown cold. Still she couldn't turn loose of it. It was her anchor—so she wouldn't fly apart in pieces like she was afraid she would. "I'll fix breakfast for you in the morning," she said.

It would be better to be busy when the time came, better to have something to focus on—even if she scorched the eggs and burned the bacon.

"No—no breakfast. I just want to say my goodbyes." Mariah blinked back tears.

She would not cry.

Luke placed his half-empty cup in the sink, then returned to the table. "I'd better go. I—I just wanted to tell you alone. And, Mariah…"

"Yes?"

"Thank you—thanks for everything you've done."

Mariah forced a smile to her lips and brushed aside his words. He leaned close to kiss her. "No, Luke," she said, her voice cracking on her words. "It—it's better this way."

If he touched his lips to hers, she could never let him leave.

He brushed his fingers across her cheek instead, a brief touch, a light touch.

But Mariah knew she would feel it for the rest of her life.

Chapter Fourteen

Luke passed all the towns he'd barely noticed on his ride west. Now they clipped by even *more* painfully—because of the woman he was leaving behind.

The goodbyes had been hard. Callie's little face had puckered until it nearly broke his heart. Una was grateful for what he'd done for her son, and Eli had given Luke's cycle a last wistful glance.

But saying goodbye to Mariah had been the hardest of all. She'd remained subdued, avoiding every emotion she could, but nonetheless he'd seen the glimmer of tears in her eyes.

And it had stabbed him in the heart.

He'd only been in Sunrise a short while, but he'd come to love them all—especially one beautiful, mixed-heritage woman with lovely green eyes and the most beautiful smile he'd ever seen.

Though today that smile had been missing.

And so had his own.

Was he doing the right thing by going back to Chicago? It didn't feel like it at the moment.

The ride was long and miserable. He took bypasses around towns and cities even though they added miles to his trip. When had he begun to dislike crowds and gridlocked traffic? When had he begun to see the beauty in the wide-open spaces?

He kept his eyes on the road ahead of him. If he struck anything—like a stray armadillo—he knew there would be no beautiful woman to come to his rescue.

That had been a once-in-a-lifetime happening.

Besides, there was only one woman like Mariah in this world. Luke had been a fortunate man to have met her, to have spent time with her. To have made love with her.

Don't go there, he warned himself. *Don't think about her velvet-soft skin, her soft, feminine scent, the way she could make you hot just looking at her.*

He even told himself there would be plenty of opportunities for sex in his future. Chicago was a big city. Women abounded, women who thought it a conquest to snag themselves a doctor. He'd met them, lots of them.

And, he remembered, pointedly avoided them. Except when he'd felt his own need. He hadn't been sure if he'd been using them, or if they'd been using him. And he supposed it didn't matter much. There'd been no love involved, only need. There'd been no promise of commitment.

Though he recalled a few of them who'd wanted to slip a noose around his bachelor neck. That was when he would plead work or some other excuse until they moved on to some other sorry sucker.

Mariah had been different.

She could easily have lassoed him with that commitment noose, and he'd no doubt have gone willingly. But Mariah didn't use wiles. She was open and honest, a woman with real feelings. When she gave her love, she'd never take it back.

When she gave her heart, it would be forever.

And Luke had to be ten kinds of an idiot to walk away from a woman like that.

A dozen times he'd been ready to turn the cycle around and head back to her. But he couldn't keep running. He had to prove he could take back the reins of his life, handle anything life threw his way, or he would never heal.

He'd told Mariah he would call, but she'd thought a clean break was best. She'd wished him good luck with his life, but when he'd tried to kiss her, she'd turned away with hurt in her eyes.

He was the second man to walk out of her life.

He was no better than Will.

And a much bigger fool.

Mariah tried to go about her days as if everything were fine—but inside she ached for the man she would never see again. Callie asked about him every day and Mariah tried to explain, but then a little while later she would ask again.

Mariah had wanted this for Luke, knew he needed to return to the trauma unit where he belonged, where he could do so much good.

Chicago was his home every bit as much as this was home to her and Callie. Luke belonged to another world, a world full of special medicines and treatments, a world full of fancy hospitals and…and sophisticated women.

Not women like her.

In fact, he'd probably already forgotten her.

And that's what hurt the most.

Una had bustled over this morning for a cup of hot herbal tea and to help Mariah with her mail-order inventory, and Mariah was happy for the company.

It took her mind off Luke.

She'd thought of little else but him the past few days—and if she was ever going to get back to her life and forget her heartache, she needed to start right now.

Today.

"Are you missing that man of yours?" Una asked when she sat down with her tea.

Una had a way of getting to the point of things fast, something Mariah had always liked about her. Just not today. And not with this point.

The mere mention of Luke brought a sheen of tears to her eyes and a lump to her throat. She'd hoped today she could start forgetting—just a little.

"Can we keep our attention on the inventory?"

Una ignored her. "You know he might have stuck around here, if you'd asked him to."

Asked him to? Mariah couldn't have done that. Luke had his life back—or at least he soon would. He might have broken her heart when he left, but he was doing what he needed to do, what he had to do—if he was to heal.

Besides, Mariah would never beg another man to stay the way she had Will. Her pride still hurt from that humiliation. But she hadn't been strong then. Now she was able to stand on her own two feet, able to take care of herself and her daughter.

They might not have a lot, but they had each other.

And that was enough.

She missed Luke every minute of every day—and she always would. But she could never ask him to give up his life there and return to Sunrise, and her. "Luke's needed at his hospital," she told Una.

"Instead of here? We needed him bad the night of Jimmy's accident. Without him, Jimmy might not have made it. We don't have many doctors—and we don't have a trauma doctor within miles. We also have a woman who could use a man in her life."

"Una, we're supposed to be going over my inventory."

Una gave her a stern look. "You don't know what's good for you, Mariah Cade."

Mariah knew what was good for her—Luke. But they belonged to very different worlds, worlds that didn't mesh. And wishing otherwise wasn't going to change a thing.

She needed to move forward with her life.

The way Luke was moving forward with his.

Luke had no home to go back to. He'd put everything he had in storage before he'd left, sold his boat, sold his Lake Shore Drive condo, so he decided to bunk at the hospital. There were rooms for the doctors on call to catch some sleep, and Luke had staked out one of them. Later, he'd look for a new condo, a town house or maybe an apartment with four walls and no atmosphere.

The staff at the med center was happy he was back and referred to his long sojourn as his recent "vacation."

Well, if it had been a vacation, Luke would soon need another one.

The trauma unit had never been busier.

He rarely got a night to sleep in that room he'd laid claim to. But that was good; Luke didn't need time on his hands or he'd start thinking about Mariah.

Dane's accident and death also haunted him in every lax moment—but Luke was trying his best to deal with it. Every day was a test of his endurance. No matter how much he wanted to he couldn't turn back time or change the outcome of that horrible night.

And if he could, was there anything he could do differently? Had he tried hard enough, done everything possible to save his son?

That was something Luke would never know.

"Phone call for you, Dr. Phillips."

"Thanks, Luanne," he said to the best nurse the trauma unit ever had. "I'll take it in the doctor's lounge." He was through until an ambulance deposited another case on his doorstep.

He picked up the phone in the lounge, realizing he was hoping it was Mariah. On the off chance that she might call him, he'd given her the phone number at the hospital, but even as he hoped, he knew it wouldn't be her on the other end.

It was late, and she would have Callie in bed, and she would either be rocking in that old swing on the front porch or getting ready for bed herself.

Bed. A sudden image of Mariah undressed and slipping between lavender-scented sheets teased at his brain. *Don't go there,* he warned himself.

He had enough images of her to get past already.

"Dr. Phillips," he said.

"Hi, Luke."

It was his dad—and Luke knew what was coming. His mother had been trying to get him to come over for dinner a half-dozen times since he'd been back—but Luke had pleaded work because he wasn't ready to answer the questions he knew were on his parents' minds.

"I'll be there, Dad. What night?" Luke didn't even need to ask why he'd called. He already knew.

"Now that's more like it. Tomorrow night—seven o'clock sharp. And no last-minute excuses, either, Luke. Your mother and I have hardly gotten to see you since you've been back."

"Dad, you know what this place is like. No promises." But he'd seriously try to be there.

The evening wasn't just dinner with his parents, but also with his sisters, their husbands and kids.

He hugged his sisters, shook hands with his brothers-in-law, arm-wrestled his nephews, except the six-month-old, kissed his nieces and ruffled their curls.

And remembered Callie.

The little girl could outshine every child here, with all her determination, her bravery. He'd been enchanted by her—and by her equally brave and determined mother.

Just thinking of them, he suddenly felt damned lonely.

They had become more like family to him than the bunch gathered here in his parents' stately suburban home.

"Luke, you're far too quiet tonight," his mother said. "Is something wrong?"

"No, Mom—I'm fine." He wasn't sure he could explain, at least not in words she could understand.

Luke wasn't sure he understood it all himself. All he knew was that he missed Mariah with a fierceness. Knew there could never be another woman for him but her. Knew he admired her, her strength, her courage, her ability to hold her world—and Callie's—together single-handedly.

She was life itself, the sun that started his day, the ache he went to bed with at night—because she wasn't there beside him.

Every minute of every hour he was tempted to hop on his cycle and ride back to her, through the hot desert heat, to hold her, taste her, breathe in her scent one more time.

What would his parents think of her, of Callie? Luke couldn't imagine anyone not finding them as special as he did, his parents included.

But Luke knew he couldn't uproot them, not when Callie blossomed under the desert sun, Mariah's herbs healing her small body, keeping her pain at bay.

Callie was strong, but she could never survive Chicago's long, blowing winters—and Mariah would miss the healing land she was so much a part of.

But could he live without Mariah in his life? Without Callie, the little girl who'd stolen his heart? Could he be a husband to Mariah? A dad to Callie?

He'd failed at one marriage already. He'd also failed Dane. No one mentioned his son, but Luke remembered Dane's place at his grandparents' table. It was now the empty chair—and Luke hurt just seeing it. The pain would never go away, but he could learn to live with it, with the memories.

Somehow Luke made it through dinner, coming up with just enough small talk that his family wouldn't worry about him. They hurt, too, because their family was minus one important member.

Luke had almost made it to the front door as everyone was leaving, when he felt his father's hand clasp him on the shoulder.

"May I have a moment with you, son?"

"How about later, Dad? I should be getting back to the hospital. The unit's been swamped lately."

"I know it's been busy. I also know how much they need you there," he said. "While you were gone—"

"Dad, they managed quite nicely without me. I've been over the E.R. records. The team did great. We could always use more help—but medicine is like that everywhere."

Luke thought about the small E.R. he and the sheriff had taken Jimmy to that night a few long weeks ago. They'd been woefully shorthanded and had welcomed Luke with open arms. Good medicine didn't just belong to the cities. The small, rural places needed it, too.

He thought about the offer the small hospital had made to him—and each lonely night without Mariah he began to wish he'd taken them up on it.

Luke followed his dad into his richly paneled study and accepted the snifter of expensive brandy the man offered him.

"You were gone a long time, son. Your mother and I were worried sick about you."

Luke sampled the brandy and felt it slide down his throat like velvet. "I know, Dad, and I'm sorry if I worried you. But after Dane's death I had...things to work out and I couldn't do it here."

"And did you work them out?"

"I'm here, aren't I?" He instantly regretted his sharp tone. He closed his eyes a moment to find his balance. He was back, but he was also miserable. "I found I can work again—and that's one thing I needed to discover. I miss my son and always will, but I'm beginning to forgive myself."

"Luke, you never had anything to forgive yourself for. Dane's injuries that night were horrific. He didn't have a chance, despite all your efforts. We miss our grand-child deeply, but you are not responsible for his death."

Luke nodded. "I'm learning to live with that now, Dad. And thanks, thanks for helping me face that and…accept it. It still hurts, though."

"Yes—and it always will. But believe in yourself, Luke."

There was someone else who believed in him. Mariah. A smile crossed his face when he thought of her. She'd wanted him to come back and face his demons.

And he had. He'd come to grips with his pain, dis-covered he still had a love of medicine—and that he could make a difference. He also discovered the trauma unit wasn't enough for him. No longer could he bury himself in work. He wanted a life *outside* medicine, too.

His dad had waited until retirement to become part of their family. His entire life had been the hospital and his career. Luke didn't blame him. He'd been going down the same road—until fate stepped in and his life changed.

"I do believe in myself, Dad."

Now.

Finally.

And Luke also knew what he wanted.

Mariah.

* * *

Everyone at the hospital wished him well and told him he would always have a job here, if he changed his mind.

Would he be returning?

Would Mariah turn him down flat?

All Luke knew was that he loved her—and if she didn't love him back, he wasn't sure his heart could bear it.

He'd left her, the way Will had done—and she might never forgive him for that. Might never trust him to stick around. But the one thing not in doubt was his love for her.

He'd just have to convince her of that.

His parents hadn't been happy he was leaving again. He'd only just returned. But they wanted happiness for their son. And Luke knew they'd be excited when they met Mariah and Callie. They'd love them as he did. How could anyone not?

But first he had to convince Mariah to marry him, convince her that he'd be a worthy husband. And Luke would do whatever it took to make her his.

He saw his last Cubs game, ate his last Chicago pizza, took his last look at Lake Michigan, and as he packed his few belongings into his saddlebags, knew he would miss none of it.

Luke climbed on his cycle and headed out of the city. The last time he'd been running *from* something— the awful memories of his failure to Dane. But this time he was running *to* something.

The woman he loved.

If she would have him.

Chapter Fifteen

Mariah was doing fine. It was the start of a new week and she'd finally gotten Luke out of her system. She'd gone an entire three minutes and forty-five seconds without crying, thinking of him or wishing he was here.

That was a new record.

Callie had been asking for a picnic by the stream. Mariah had put it off because she wasn't certain she could handle the reminders of Luke that the place evoked.

But she knew she couldn't avoid the spot forever. Besides, everything on her property reminded her of Luke. Maybe that was why it was so hard to forget him.

"Are we ready, Mommy?" Callie asked for the third time in the last ten minutes.

"I just need to put in our tablecloth and napkins—then we're ready."

Callie was excited—and Mariah hoped she could

keep up the charade and not spoil her daughter's day. She added the last two items to the hamper and they set off for the stream. Mariah pasted on a smile she hoped she could keep in place—for Callie's sake.

She avoided a glance at the cabin as they angled off toward the picnic spot. Early one morning she'd stripped the sheets from the old bed, then sank down on the bare mattress, feeling the tears come to her eyes. The sheets still carried Luke's scent and she'd buried her face in them and drank in his essence.

That had been the hardest day so far, but she knew there were many more to come. She'd hoped the pain would subside over time, but how long would it take? Three years? Five years?

A lifetime?

Callie gamboled ahead of her. "No playing in the stream today," Mariah reminded.

The last two days Callie had complained of joint pain, not in her legs but other joints, and Mariah couldn't let her catch a chill. She'd increased some of Callie's herbal medications, which had helped somewhat, but Mariah was fearful of what was yet to come with her child's disease.

She'd been tempted to call Luke and ask if his hospital had a medicine that could help. Mariah would rush Callie there if it took every last penny she had. He'd given her his number at the hospital, which she'd tucked away in her lingerie drawer, praying she'd have the strength not to take it out and call. At least, not for herself. For Callie, only for Callie, would she even think of using it.

Today, though, Callie seemed better. But Mariah was afraid to ease up on her precautions—and staying out of the water was number one on her list.

She spread out the blanket on the grass and set out their sandwiches and fruit, along with a cup of milk for Callie and an iced tea for herself. She'd almost put in a bottle of wine but knew it would remind her of Luke and the picnics they'd shared. And Mariah already had enough reminders to deal with.

Callie loosened her braces and sat down next to Mariah. "I wish Luke was here," she said. "He liked our picnics, didn't he, Mommy?"

Mariah tested the ready smile she'd brought along and hoped it held. "Yes, he liked them," she said.

"Will he come back when all the patients get well at his hospital? I want to show him what I can do on my play gym."

It was just this sort of question she'd been fielding from her daughter since Luke had left three weeks ago. And Mariah was no closer to coming up with an answer that would satisfy Callie—or herself—since then.

"Remember, we talked about this, sweetheart. Luke lives far away. He *can't* come back."

"I bet he *wants* to," Callie added.

Mariah couldn't speak. Tears clogged her throat. She wished that Callie was right. But she knew it was only her daughter's wishful thinking. Luke couldn't give up all he'd worked for. He could do so much good at the hospital——and it would be selfish to want him here with her.

Mariah talked about everything she could think of with Callie during their lunch—except Luke. How could time go by so slowly? Every daylight hour seemed like two, every nighttime hour stretched like eternity.

At night she tried chamomile tea to help her sleep—

but it hadn't lessened her insomnia. She'd lain awake, tossing and turning and thinking about Luke.

"Are you ready for your story now?" she asked Callie after they'd finished eating.

"I'm ready," Callie said, and curled up next to Mariah.

The sun glinted through the boughs of the tree, the wind rustling its leaves. The spot was peaceful, idyllic— and Mariah felt rich indeed. Only one thing was missing—a man to enjoy it with her. *One* man. Luke.

When they were finished reading, Callie helped gather up their things, and they started back up the hill to the house. Mariah was quiet, Luke very much on her mind. Her daughter reached up and put a small hand in hers. "It's okay, Mommy," she said. "I miss him, too."

Mariah smiled through her pain and drew Callie close to her side.

She'd have to try acting lessons if she intended to hide her feelings from her daughter.

It was a hot August day but Mariah needed a fresh supply of herbs if she was going to fill all her mail orders.

Una had suggested several new ones that could help Callie if Mariah could find them. The child was doing well again, but the recent flare-up had worried Mariah, and she wanted to have every medicine possible in her small arsenal if the need arose.

Mariah parked the old truck in her usual place and set out to search for what she needed. Una was watching Callie for her, but Mariah didn't want to be gone too long. The hot day didn't lend itself to a long outing anyway.

She soon had gathered her customary herbs, enough to fill her standing orders, but the ones she'd hoped to find for Callie still eluded her—arnica, pepper root and a certain kind of willow bark that Una had suggested. She'd have to search the mesa, the one place she'd hoped to avoid, the place where she'd first met Luke.

She swallowed hard and trod up the path. Luke was a lifetime away—but she felt his presence every bit as much as if he were here physically. The heat of the sun beat down as she searched among the rocks for any sign of the plants she needed. She found a tiny arnica plant, a fledgling one, but with the flowers she needed, and Mariah added it to her basket.

She wiped the sweat from her forehead and glanced down at the quiet road below. She remembered the day Luke had stopped for shade. How handsome he'd looked, how rugged, his eyes matching the Arizona sky above her. She wondered about him, what he was doing, if he was all right.

If he missed her even a little.

Her heart ached to see him again—even for a moment. Her body needed his touch, just a caress, maybe a kiss. But she knew that would only make things worse.

Then she spotted the red pods of a pepper plant growing hardily out of the rocky soil. She knelt and dug carefully around it with her trowel. Perfect, she pronounced, holding it up and admiring its roots. This one small plant would yield plenty of the medicine she needed and she tucked it in her basket, pleased with her find.

That's when she heard it—a sound in the distance, like the rumble of thunder from a coming storm. But it wasn't thunder. It was the sound of a motorcycle.

Luke, she thought.

Then she dismissed the idea as foolishness. Luke was miles away. In Chicago. In his hospital. Where he'd gone to make peace with the past. Where he could do so much good.

The sun above struck the metal of the oncoming bike and reflected off it, nearly blinding her. She shaded her eyes and tried to see the rider. Then her heart lodged in her throat.

It was Luke.

She was sure of it.

He pulled to the side of the road, spewing red dust in his wake, then dismounted and glanced up the mesa—to where Mariah stood.

Her heart thudded and her breath came in shallow gasps. What was he doing here? Why had he come back?

She started down the mesa, tripping along the trail, expecting Luke and the cycle to be a mirage, one that would cruelly disappear as she neared.

But this was not a mirage.

Luke was real.

She was nearly to him when she stopped, afraid if she took one step closer she'd throw herself into his arms. "What…what are you doing here?" she asked.

A small grin edged at his mouth. "I don't suppose you'd believe I stopped for shade?"

She gave him a frown.

"I missed you, Mariah," he said.

She closed her eyes and let the sound of his voice wash over her. She'd missed him, too. So much that she ached from it. She'd wanted him to come back, had wished it a thousand times. Had those wishes conjured him up?

"Luke, I—"

Mariah couldn't think. She didn't understand what all this meant. Her basket wobbled and her herbs tumbled out. She needed them, all of them, for her daughter. There. Now her brain was beginning to function again.

She reached down to gather them up, but Luke was ahead of her, his hands stilling hers. "I'll get them."

And then he was kissing her. His mouth felt so wonderful, so familiar.

"I need the herbs for Callie—be careful of them," she said when he'd finally quit kissing her and began picking up her hodgepodge of plants.

"I am," he said. He picked up every last one and placed them carefully in her basket, then took her hand and led her toward the cycle. "Can you ride behind me as far as your truck?"

She swore she'd never get on that bike again—any bike. But her truck was so far away and her legs were too wobbly to walk. She nodded. "Just to my truck—not an inch farther."

He tied a large blue bandanna over the basket, then hooked it onto the handlebars and climbed aboard the bike. Mariah got on behind and told him where she'd left her ancient truck.

She wrapped her arms around his middle and tried to ignore the closeness of their bodies. This was just a lift to her truck, then she'd drive home and sort out all this in her mind.

When she could finally think.

* * *

"Now—explain, Luke Phillips."

Mariah looked like a loaded six-shooter ready to blast away at him before he could even tell her that he loved her, madly, totally, *forever*.

Was she ready to trust a man who'd ridden out of her life?

Luke hoped so.

The sun had already set, and the dark had marched in by the time Mariah had Callie asleep and joined him on the porch. He rocked the swing in a measured rhythm, but Mariah refused to join him there.

Instead she stood her ground a few feet away.

Afraid.

He could read that in her face.

He got up from the swing. He could think better when he paced—so he paced the big porch that seemed to have shrunk in the last few minutes.

"I went back to Chicago, to the trauma unit, working day and night—more hours than I wanted to. I was able to put aside my memories of Dane, of the night he died. Not that I can ever forget him. I can't, Mariah. He'll always be a part of my life—but I learned to forgive myself."

She glanced up and he saw tears shimmering in her eyes, a soft smile on her lips. He knew it was what she'd wanted for him. Without her he'd never have accomplished it, though. He owed everything to her. Everything that he was now, everything that he could be.

"I came back because I love you, Mariah. I want you by my side—always. You and Callie."

She looked away and Luke thought he saw her

usually strong shoulders tremble. "I can't leave here, Luke. You know that. This is where Callie thrives."

Luke went to her and tipped up her chin so he could look into her eyes, so she could read the intent in his. "I know that, sweetheart. I want you by my side, *here*."

"Here? But, Luke, there's nothing here. We don't have a trauma center or even much of a hospital."

"That's something I can change, Mariah. The hospital offered me a position before I left here, but I wasn't sure I could be a doctor anymore. I had to go back to Chicago. I had to know. You made me realize that."

She turned away from him, her shoulders clearly shaking now. He wanted to pull her close, hold her until she stopped trembling. But she needed reassurance, not comfort.

"I found out I still have a lot to offer," he told her. "I want the job, Mariah. To be the new chief of trauma for this area."

She spun around to face him. He tried to read the expression on her face, in her eyes, but there was such a mixture of emotions he couldn't be sure what he saw.

"It won't mean anything, though. Nothing will mean anything—unless you'll be my wife."

"You want to…marry me?"

She wrapped her arms around herself as if she were cold. But the fall evening was warm. The stars were out in all their celestial beauty.

"Yes, I want to marry you." Then he rubbed his jaw, irked at himself. "I, uh, guess I forgot the most important part. I don't propose often, so forgive me. I forgot to say…*I love you*."

Her eyes widened; a very hesitant smile came to her sweet lips.

"Oh, Luke, I love you, too. With all my heart."

She went into his arms and Luke held her in an embrace he'd dreamed about every mile of his ride back here. He raised her chin and kissed her sweet mouth and was sure he'd never tasted anything more wonderful.

"So, is that a yes—will you marry me?"

A wide smile tilted at her mouth. "Yes, Luke, I'll marry you, on one condition."

Luke hesitated. "What's the condition?"

"That Callie approves."

He smiled down at her. "I think I can win her over."

"I think you can, too."

Mariah hadn't been able to sleep last night. That must have been why she'd overslept this morning—until Callie shook her awake.

"Mommy, my school starts today."

Ohmigosh!

Mariah had been so surprised by Luke's proposal that she'd totally forgotten this was Callie's big day. In fact, she had to pinch herself to be certain she hadn't dreamed the whole thing.

But that didn't help the moment. She'd planned to fix Callie a good breakfast, help her dress in her pretty new school dress—

Dress.

Callie was already wearing her new pretty dress. Her barrettes were in place. And her long hair was braided, a matching bow at the end of it. How? "Callie—"

"Go back to sleep, Mommy. Luke fixed my break-fast—and he's going to walk me to school."

Mariah pressed her fingers to her temples. Luke. He seemed to have turned their world upside-down in less than twenty-four hours. She supposed she should be glad he wasn't riding her to school on his bike.

"Want a kiss, Mommy?"

She smiled at her daughter, who was growing up, starting first grade in the small, rural school. Callie was beautiful. Her child. And Mariah loved her so much.

She gave her a squeeze and a kiss. "You hold on to Luke's hand," she said. "And I'll be there to pick you up this afternoon."

"I know, Mommy."

"Where's *my* kiss?"

Mariah knew the sound of that voice. She loved the man it belonged to—and always would.

"Luke, you're not staying at school," Callie said with a giggle. "You don't get a kiss."

"Have a fun day, sweetheart," she said to Callie.

Then when they left, she collapsed back onto her pillow with only one thought on her mind.

Luke loved her.

Luke was ready for his interview. He sported a fresh pair of chinos and a pressed blue shirt—pressed by his saddlebags. He needed to move out of that cabin.

It was no place for the new trauma chief to live.

Which was exactly what he told Mariah when he showed up at her back door this morning.

"I'm taking you and Callie to Rudy's for pizza

tonight to celebrate my new job," he added and planted a kiss on her cheek.

"Luke—what has Callie said?"

He smiled. "She wants to marry me, too."

Mariah gave his chest a playful shove. "Luke, be serious."

"She asked if I was going to be her daddy."

"And what did you say?"

"That I was going to be her daddy just as soon as I could talk her mommy into setting a wedding date." He planted a kiss on her full, sultry lips, then another and another. "Now when will it be?"

"How about as soon as possible?"

"Too long," he said and kissed her again.

"Luke, weddings don't happen by themselves. It takes a little planning at the very least."

"How much planning?"

Mariah laughed at the worried look on his face. She loved this man, knew when she saw him standing there in the doorway with Callie all ready for school that she would always love him.

A man who could tie a bow in Callie's hair with such care would stick around and be a husband forever.

And forever was what she wanted with Luke.

"We need at least a week," she said, knowing he'd accept nothing longer than that.

"Okay—one week. No more. I'm an impatient man."

She kissed him soundly and pushed him toward the door. "Go to your interview, Luke Phillips. I have a wedding to plan."

Epilogue

Luke was determined Mariah would have a fairy-tale wedding, the wedding of her dreams. But Mariah had her dream *man*; she couldn't care less about the wedding part.

The entire town was invited, along with Luke's parents, his three sisters with their families and half a dozen of his closest friends. Sunrise would be bulging at the seams.

The old church was Una's domain and she shooed even the priest away while she handled the decorations. The reception afterward was slated for the church hall, not that it would hold more than fifty people at a time. That, too, was Una's territory and she told Mariah not to worry, the overflow crowd could filter outdoors.

She and the ladies of the town were handling the food for the buffet and Luke was supplying the champagne. It wasn't every day that Sunrise had a wedding.

And the town would be talking about this one for a long time to come—or until the first baby came.

Luke wanted children, saying that Mariah was a natural-born mother, and he wanted the chance to be a father to Callie and as many more babies as she'd agree to have.

Mariah still occasionally saw the pain in his eyes—but not the haunted shadows. He would always miss his son, would always carry the sadness in his heart—but he had come to accept that no one could have saved his child that night.

As the new chief of the trauma unit he had the chance to save others—and that would be some balm for his soul.

Callie was Mariah's maid of honor, quite an honor for a six-year-old. Callie thought so, too, and kept wanting to try on her pretty dress so she could hear the satin of the skirt rustle.

"Out! Out!" Una scolded as Luke tried to come into the bedroom. "You won't get to see your bride before the ceremony."

Luke rolled his eyes, but wisely backed out of the room.

Mariah had to laugh. "Una, he may never speak to you again."

"I'll worry about that later," she retorted. "Now, let me get you into that dress."

The sleek white gown had a million tiny buttons down the back, lined up like a row of marching soldiers. Mariah just hoped Una's old fingers could manage them.

The gown had been a terrible extravagance, but Luke had insisted this was a celebration.

And it was.

A celebration of their love for each other. He was hers forever, as she was his.

And always would be.

"What time is it?" she asked Una, suddenly realizing she'd been daydreaming.

"It's not quite time to leave for the church yet. Now quit all that fidgeting and let me get these flowers in your hair," the old woman ordered officiously.

Una had brushed Mariah's hair until it gleamed and now added the small cluster of fall wildflowers to it. Her bridal bouquet would be a larger version of the same collected flowers.

Finally Una pronounced her ready and they left for the church in a fancy rented car. Mariah supposed her old truck wouldn't have been up to the mission.

Callie had ridden along with them. Mariah marveled at how beautiful her little girl looked. Her smile was exuberant. Callie was wild about Luke—and thrilled she'd now have a daddy.

Mariah had met Luke's parents for the first time yesterday—and she liked them. They adored Callie, as did Luke's sisters and their husbands. And Callie loved playing with her new cousins. Luke's sisters were a bit possessive when it came to their brother—and Mariah understood why. Luke was a good man—and they were determined to make sure he was happy.

Mariah heard the music as they drove up to the front of the church. A few worried townsfolk stood outside, waiting for the bride to arrive. The men raced forward to open the car door for her and escorted her up the steps.

Mariah felt like a princess with her own footmen—and

she had to suppress a giggle. The entire day seemed like a dream scenario—with the real prize at the end of it.

Luke.

Mrs. Charley presided at the organ, and when she spotted the bride, she quickly segued into the "Wedding March" and the entire church stood. Callie stood in front of her, ready for her trip down the aisle. And there at the front, standing next to Father DeVargas, was Luke.

Mariah's heart knocked in rhythm with her knees.

He looked so gorgeous in his black tux, and she saw the hint of a smile on his lips. His eyes stayed riveted on her face as she made her way down the aisle behind Callie.

He took her hand when she reached him, and his blue eyes shimmered with the same love she had for him. Together they turned and faced Father DeVargas— and Mariah knew she could never be happier than she was this day.

Luke was hers forever.

And she was his.

Smiles greeted them as they fairly ran down the aisle and out into the beautiful Arizona sunshine—and all the happiness they could ever want.

* * * * *

Welcome to cowboy country...

Turn the page for a sneak preview of
TEXAS BABY
by
Kathleen O'Brien
An exciting new title from
Harlequin Superromance for everyone
who loves stories about the West.

Harlequin Superromance—
Where life and love weave together in emotional and
unforgettable ways.

CHAPTER ONE

CHASE TRANSFERRED his gaze to the road and identified a foreign spot on the horizon. A car. Almost half a mile away, where the straight, tree-lined drive met the public road. He could tell it was coming too fast, but judging the speed of a vehicle moving straight toward you was tricky.

It wasn't until it was about two hundred yards away that he realized the driver must be drunk...or crazy. Or both.

The guy was going maybe sixty. On a private drive, out here in ranch country, where kids or horses or tractors or stupid chickens might come darting out any minute, that was criminal. Chase straightened from his comfortable slouch and waved his hands.

"Slow down, you fool," he called out. He took the porch steps quickly and began walking fast down the driveway.

The car veered oddly, from one lane to another, then

up onto the slight rise of the thick green spring grass. It just barely missed the fence.

"Slow down, damn it!"

He couldn't see the driver, and he didn't recognize this automobile. It was small and old, and couldn't have cost much even when it was new. It was probably white, but now it needed either a wash or a new paint job or both.

"Damn it, what's wrong with you?"

At the last minute, he had to jump away, because the idiot behind the wheel clearly wasn't going to turn to avoid a collision. He couldn't believe it. The car kept coming, finally slowing a little, but it was too late.

Still going about thirty miles an hour, it slammed into the large, white-brick pillar that marked the front boundaries of the house. The pillar wasn't going to give an inch, so the car had to. The front end folded up like a paper fan.

It seemed to take forever for the car to settle, as if the trauma happened in slow motion, reverberating from the front to the back of the car in ripples of destruction. The front windshield suddenly seemed to ice over with lethal bits of glassy frost. Then the side windows exploded.

The front driver's door wrenched open, as if the car wanted to expel its contents. Metal buckled hideously. Small pieces, like hubcaps and mirrors, skipped and ricocheted insanely across the oyster-shell driveway.

Finally, everything was still. Into the silence, a plume of steam shot up like a geyser, smelling of rust and heat. Its snakelike hiss almost smothered the low, agonized moan of the driver.

Chase's anger had disappeared. He didn't feel anything but a dull sense of disbelief. Things like this didn't happen in real life. Not in his life. Maybe the sun had actually put him to sleep….

But he was already kneeling beside the car. The driver was a woman. The frosty glass-ice of the windshield was dotted with small flecks of blood. She must have hit it with her head, because just below her hairline a red liquid was seeping out. He touched it. He tried to wipe it away before it reached her eyebrow, though, of course that made no sense at all. Her eyes were shut.

Was she conscious? Did he dare move her? Her dress was covered in glass, and the metal of the car was sticking out lethally in all the wrong places.

Then he remembered, with an intense relief, that every good medical man in the county was here, just behind the house, drinking his champagne. He found his phone and paged Trent.

The woman moaned again.

Alive, then. Thank God for that.

He saw Trent coming toward him, starting out at a lope, but quickly switching to a full run.

"Get Dr. Marchant," Chase called. "Don't bother with 911."

Trent didn't take long to assess the situation. A fraction of a second, and he began pulling out his cell phone and running toward the house.

The yelling seemed to have roused the woman. She opened her eyes. They were blue and clouded with pain and confusion.

"Chase," she said.

His breath stalled. His head pulled back. "What?"

Her only answer was another moan, and he wondered if he had imagined the word. He reached around her and put his arm behind her shoulders. She was tiny. Probably petite by nature, but surely way too thin. He could feel her shoulder blades pushing against her skin, as fragile as the wishbone in a turkey.

She seemed to have passed out, so he put his other arm under her knees and lifted her out. He tried to avoid the jagged metal, but her skirt caught on a piece and the tearing sound seemed to wake her again.

"No," she said. "Please."

"I'm just trying to help," he said. "It's going to be all right."

She seemed profoundly distressed. She wriggled in his arms, and she was so weak, like a broken bird. It made him feel too big and brutish. And intrusive. As if touching her this way, his bare hands against the warm skin behind her knees, were somehow a transgression.

He wished he could be more delicate. But he smelled gasoline, and he knew it wasn't safe to leave her here.

Finally he heard the sound of voices, as guests began to run around the side of the house, alerted by Trent. Dr. Marchant was at the front, racing toward them as if he were forty instead of seventy. Susannah was right behind him, her green dress floating around her trim legs.

"Please," the woman in his arms murmured again. She looked at him, the expression in her blue eyes lost and bewildered. He wondered if she might be on drugs. Hitting her head on the windshield might account for this unfocused, glazed look, but it couldn't explain the crazy driving.

"Please, put me down. Susannah… The wedding…"

Chase's arms tightened instinctively, and he froze in

his tracks. She whimpered, and he realized he might be hurting her. "Say that again?"

"The wedding. I have to stop it."

* * * * *

Be sure to look for TEXAS BABY,
available September 11, 2007,
as well as other fantastic Superromance titles
available in September.

Welcome to Cowboy Country...

TEXAS BABY

by *Kathleen O'Brien*

#1441

Chase Clayton doesn't know what to think.
A beautiful stranger has just crashed his
engagement party, demanding that he not
marry because she's pregnant with his baby.
But the kicker is—he's never seen her before.

Look for TEXAS BABY and other fantastic
Superromance titles on sale September 2007.

Available wherever books are sold.

The latest novel in The Lakeshore Chronicles
by *New York Times* bestselling author

SUSAN WIGGS

From the award-winning author of *Summer at Willow Lake*
comes an unforgettable story of a woman's emotional journey
from the heartache of the past to hope for the future.

With her daughter grown and flown, Nina Romano is ready to
embark on a new adventure. She's waited a long time for dating,
travel and chasing dreams. But just as she's beginning to enjoy
being on her own, she finds herself falling for Greg Bellamy,
owner of the charming Inn at Willow Lake and a single father
with two kids of his own.

DOCKSIDE

"The perfect summer read." —Debbie Macomber

*Available the first week of August 2007
wherever paperbacks are sold!*

REQUEST YOUR FREE BOOKS!

2 FREE NOVELS PLUS 2 FREE GIFTS!

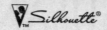

SPECIAL EDITION®

Life, Love and Family!

SSE07

Bailey DelMonico has finally
gotten her life on track, and is
passionate about her recent career
change. Nothing will stand in the way
of her becoming a doctor...that is,
until she's paired with the sharp-tongued
Dr. Ivan Munro.

Watch the sparks fly in

Doctor in
the House

by *USA TODAY* Bestselling Author
Marie Ferrarella

Available September 2007

Intrigued? Read more at
TheNextNovel.com

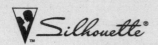

COMING NEXT MONTH

SPECIAL EDITION

#1849 BACHELOR NO MORE—Victoria Pade
Northbridge Nuptials
Shock #1: Mara Pratt's sweet, elderly coworker led a double life—decades ago, she'd run off with a bank robber and was now facing hard time! Shock #2: The woman's grandson, corporate raider Jared Perry, was back in Northbridge to help Grandma, and he saw Mara as a tempting takeover target—trying to steal her heart at every turn!

#1850 HER BEST MAN—Crystal Green
Montana Mavericks: Striking It Rich
Years ago, DJ Traub had been best man at his brother's wedding to Allaire Buckman—but secretly DJ had wanted to be the groom, so he'd left town to avoid further heartbreak. Now the rich restaurateur had returned to Thunder Canyon and into the orbit of the still alluring, long-divorced Allaire. Had he become the best man...to share Allaire's life?

#1851 THE OTHER SISTER—Lynda Sandoval
Return to Troublesome Gulch
Long after tragedy had taken his best friend in high school, paramedic Brody Austin was finally ready to work through his own feelings of guilt. That's when he ran into his best friend's kid sister, Faith Montesantos. All grown up, the pretty, vivacious high school counselor helped him reconcile with the past and move on...to a future in her arms.

#1852 DAD IN DISGUISE—Kate Little
Baby Daze
When wealthy architect Jack Sawyer tried to "cancel" his sperm donation, he discovered his baby had already been born to single mother Rachel Reilly. So Jack went undercover as a handyman at her house to make sure his son was all right. Jack fell for the boy...and fell for Rachel—hard. But when daddy took off his disguise, would all hell break loose?

#1853 WHAT MAKES A FAMILY?—Nicole Foster
Past betrayal and loss made teacher Laurel Tanner shy away from love at every turn. And Cort Morente was hardly an eligible bachelor—he was focused on rebuilding his own life, not on romance. But their shared concern for a troubled child was about to bring them together in ways they'd never dreamed possible....

#1854 THE DEBUTANTE'S SECOND CHANCE—
Liz Flaherty
When journalist Micah Walker took over his hometown paper, the top local story was former debutante Landy Wisdom. Domestic abuse had left Landy broken—her selfless help for other victims had left her unbowed. Could Micah give her a second chance at love...or would she turn the tables and give *him* a chance—to finally find true happiness?